Full Speed Ahead

My Journey with Kit

by Valerie Tripp

Published by American Girl Publishing
Copyright © 2014 American Girl

Questions or comments? Call 1-800-845-0005, visit **americangirl.com**,
or write to Customer Service, American Girl,
8400 Fairway Place, Middleton, WI 53562.

Printed in China
14 15 16 17 18 19 20 LEO 10 9 8 7 6 5 4 3 2 1

Cover image by Michael Dwornik and Juliana Kolesova

Cataloging-in-Publication Data available from the Library of Congress

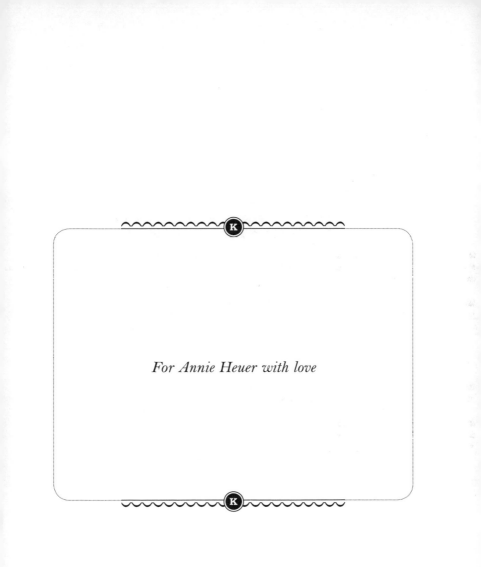

For Annie Heuer with love

Beforever

Beforever is about making connections.
It's about exploring the past, finding your
place in the present, and thinking about the
possibilities your future can bring. And it's about
seeing the common thread that ties girls from
all times together. The inspiring characters you
will meet stand up for what they care about
most: Helping others. Protecting the earth.
Overcoming injustice. Through their courageous
stories, discover how staying true to your own
beliefs will help make your world better
today—and tomorrow.

A Journey Begins

This book is about Kit, but it's also about a girl like you who travels back in time to Kit's world of 1933. You, the reader, get to decide what happens in the story. The choices you make will lead to different journeys and new discoveries.

When you reach a page in this book that asks you to make a decision, choose carefully. The decisions you make will lead to different endings. (Hint: Use a pencil to check off your choices. That way, you'll never read the same story twice.)

Want to try another ending? Go back to a choice point and find out what happens when you make different choices.

Before your journey ends, take a peek into the past, on page 188, to discover more about Kit's time.

Beep, bee-dle-lee beep beep, beep beep. It's my phone. My best friend Isabel has just sent me a photo of her pet bunny, Pippa. She is *so cute*.

I call Isabel. "Pippa is adorable," I say. "You are so lucky, Izza! I've asked my mom a million times to let me have a pet."

"And?" Isabel asks.

I sigh. "Sometimes she jokes that my room is so messy a pet would get lost in it. And sometimes she's serious and says that having a pet is a big deal and I'm not responsible enough."

Isabel says, "You were responsible about going to that science day camp thingy this summer—"

"Camp Mosquito!" That's what I called it, anyway. I still have a constellation of bites on my leg in the shape of the Big Dipper.

"You went every day even though you don't especially like creepy-crawlies like bugs or worms."

"Or *sssnakessss*," I hiss.

Isabel giggles. "And I bet you've been responsible about writing that essay for the first day of school tomorrow, right?"

Uh-oh.

"The *what*?" I gulp. "For *when*?"

"The essay," says Isabel, "due tomorrow."

Terrific. Fifth grade starts tomorrow, and I'm already behind.

Isabel goes on. "You're supposed to write a paragraph about the most important idea you learned this summer."

"Seriously? That's the most boring topic in the world! What did you write about?"

"Pippa," says Isabel, "and how pets teach us about love. Hey! I know what—you could write about Camp Mosquito."

"Mmm-hmm," I say. "How's this?" I put on a deep voice and pretend I'm reading aloud. "The most important idea I learned at science camp is that bug spray isn't repellent but Harry Sharma is. The end."

"Poor you," says Isabel. "You had to put up with Harry Sharma *and* creepy-crawlies this summer." Harry Sharma is this boy in our class at school. I couldn't believe it when he showed up at my summer camp, too. Of all the bad luck!

Isabel giggles mischievously. "You know Harry only teases you to get your attention, because he has a crush on you."

"Ee-ew!" I protest. "News flash: Harry Sharma is obnoxious and stuck-up and annoying," I tell her, leaving no room for argument. "Listen, Izza, I'd better go. If I start now and write all night long, I *might* get a paragraph written by dawn."

"Okay," Isabel says. "Call me later?"

"Of course," I say. "Bye."

❧ *Turn to page 4.*

I wander into the kitchen to make a snack, thinking about Isabel and how she and her big noisy family are crammed into a teeny house, while I'm an only child rattling around in this humongous super-sleek apartment with my mom—when my mom is here, which she usually isn't. Most of the time, like right now, she's at work. So it's just Sophie the babysitter and me.

I wave to Sophie as I walk through the living room. She gives me a brief smile but keeps on texting, ignoring me as usual. I think: *If I had a dog, I wouldn't feel so lonely.* Before I turn on the kitchen light, I look out the window. Mom and I live on the top floor of our high-rise, and the walls of our apartment are glass. It's not what you'd call cozy, but I like our apartment at times like right now, when I have a bird's-eye view of the city spread out below me, and lights are twinkling from every building around me. It's as if there's a soft, starry night sky above me *and* below me, and the starry skies meet at the horizon. It gives me a restless, shivery feeling.

I open the refrigerator and see a microwave-safe dish wrapped in plastic with a note from Mom on it:

Heat for 5 minutes.
Early bed. School tomorrow!
Love and kisses, Mom ☺

Haiku, if you don't count the smiley face. I sort of
forgot about dinner, and now it's too late to eat it, so
I just grab an apple and go back to my room.

My desk is too messy to sit at because I left my
grungy softball glove and tennis racket and balls and
socks and towels and about a hundred books on it.
(I love to read.) I take my laptop and sit on the floor.
I type:

The Most Important Idea I Learned This Summer

I stare at that, but I can't think of anything to write
except: *I wish I had a dog.*

Mom always turns the air-conditioning to subzero,
so my room is as cold as an iceberg. I grab an old coat
out of my project suitcase and snuggle into it. My project suitcase is full of old clothes I'm planning to work
on. That's my hobby: going to thrift stores and buying
old, vintage clothes. Some of the clothes—like the coat,

which I think is from the 1950s—are so cool that I wear them as is. Others I cut apart and reassemble in a totally new way for myself. I know it's a useless kind of hobby, just sort of silly and frivolous. But I don't inflict my creations on anyone, and Mom doesn't seem to mind. She says I'm fearless with the scissors.

In my project suitcase I also find an odd, heavy, rectangular sort of box. It's a camera—a *really* old-fashioned one. It's funky, but cool, with a leather strap. It must have come with a box of clothes; I don't remember buying it. Carefully, I open it up and look down at it into the viewing slot, as if I'm taking a photo. I wonder if it works—does it even have film in it? Slowly, I press the shutter button . . . *click.*

And then,

and then,

and then . . .

I realize it sounds weird and impossible, but the next thing I know, it's broad daylight, I'm in the leafy front yard of a big house, camera still in hand, and a girl who's about my age is walking toward me. And just as weird, right next to me there's a wiggly golden retriever puppy, acting as though he belongs to me and

is my best buddy. I pick him up and hold him. If this is a dream, it's a dream come true about the puppy.

"Hi," says the girl, smiling politely. She's wearing an adorable flower-print dress that I love because it's genuine-looking vintage.

"Hi," I croak.

"I'm Kit Kittredge," says the girl. "We've been expecting you. You must be Cousin Lucille."

"Lucille?" I repeat. "No." I want to say that I'm not Kit's cousin, and that Lucille is not my name, but I just stammer, "Lu . . . Lu—"

"Oh, okay, I'll call you Lulu if you want," Kit says.

Lulu? Why not? When something's so extreme that it's crazy, don't you call it a lulu? This experience I'm having right now is definitely a lulu.

Kit reaches out and scratches the puppy behind the ears. "Hi there," Kit says to him. She smiles at me, and this time her smile is big and genuine, not stiff and polite like before. "What's your dog's name?"

"He isn't my dog," I tell her. "I don't know who he belongs to."

The puppy licks me on the chin. "He sure seems to think that he belongs to you," Kit says with a grin. "He

has no collar or tags. So unless someone comes along to claim him, it looks like he's yours if you want him."

"Oh, I do!" I exclaim. "I want a dog more than anything!"

Kit nods. It's clear that she understands completely. "So what are you going to call him?" she asks.

"Buddy," I say. It's the name I've always imagined for my dog, ever since I was little, because that's what I want a dog for—to be my buddy.

"Buddy," says Kit. "That's a cute name. I have a dog named Grace. I love her like crazy. Come on inside and meet her. Everyone will be glad that you're here."

❊ *To go in and meet Grace,*
   turn to page 20.

❊ *To tell Kit I'm not Cousin Lucille,*
   turn to page 11.

I blink a bit, feeling slightly dizzy.

"Would you like to hang up your coat?" Kit asks me, pointing to a row of hooks.

"Um, sure," I say, trying to act calm and normal. I put the camera on the little table as I take off my coat.

Kit gets excited when she sees the camera. "Oh, do you like to take photos?" she asks. "So do I! I'm going to be a reporter when I grow up." Kit puts her hand on my camera and starts to pick it up.

"NO!" I shout, lunging for the camera and snatching it away from Kit. Who knows what would happen if Kit clicked the camera and was transported away, as I was? "Don't touch the camera!" I bark. "Not ever!" Then I add a feeble "Please."

Kit steps back and puts both hands up. "Okay!" she says. "Sorry."

I'm sorry, too. Oh, how I wish I could tell Kit why I didn't want her to touch the camera! But how would I explain that the camera seems to be a time-travel machine? She would think I was a total nutcase! Besides, I don't understand it myself. For all I know, Kit would be transported to my time, and I'd be left here in 1933 with no camera to help me go home, ever. And who

knows what would happen to Buddy, with whom I am already in love.

Kit can tell that I'm upset. "I understand," she says kindly. "Cameras are fragile, and expensive."

I shoot her a grateful smile as I loop the camera strap over my head so that I'm wearing the camera like a heavy necklace. I will NEVER take it off.

❈ *Turn to page 14.*

K it," I say, "wait a minute. I don't think I should go inside with you. I'm . . . I'm not your cousin Lucille."

For a second, Kit looks puzzled. Then her face softens with sympathy and she says, "Ah, I see. You're a hobo. Well, you—"

"Kit?" someone interrupts. A slender, pretty woman appears behind Kit. When she sees me, she looks distressed. "Not another one," she sighs. "And so young, too."

"Mother," says Kit, "this is Lulu and her dog, Buddy."

I'm about to explain that Lulu is not my name, but Kit's mother is already speaking to me. "You and your dog must be hot and thirsty, Lulu. It's a long walk up here from the train yard." She turns to Kit. "Give Lulu and her dog some water from the spigot by the garden. I'll meet you out there with some food."

"Please, Mother," Kit begins, "couldn't we invite—"

"No, Kit," her mother says firmly. "She's the third hobo this week. We'll give her food and then send her on her way."

Kit nods sadly, and her mother leaves.

So it looks as if Kit and her mother are going to call

me Lulu. That's okay. But it's not so cool that they think I'm a hobo. Isn't that a homeless person? Where am I? What has happened to me?

Buddy is dancing happily at my feet, and I see that he has a newspaper in his mouth. "Good boy!" I praise him. As I take the newspaper from him, I catch a glimpse of the date on it: It's September 1, 1933.

What?! Has the camera transported me back in time? I clicked the camera . . . and now I'm having some sort of *time travel* experience?

No way.

The newspaper headline is about President Franklin Roosevelt. I know he was president during World War Two, because I saw a movie about him. And one time I wrote a book report about his wife, Eleanor, but all I remember is that she helped poor people.

"Uh, excuse me," I say to Kit. "Is today's date September first, 1933?"

"Yes," says Kit. "School will be starting next week." She takes the newspaper from me. "I'll put this inside," she says. "You go around to the back of the house, and my mom and I will meet you there."

"Okay," I say, as Kit leaves.

My brain's whirling. I'm thinking, *Let me get this straight. Not only have I traveled back in time, but I'm now a homeless person! Thanks a lot, camera!*

Okay, I *am* wearing an old coat, pre-distressed cutoff jeans, and a pre-faded plaid shirt; they're very trendy in the twenty-first century, but I guess they look old and tattered to 1930s folk. Still! Why couldn't I have traveled back to being an explorer, or a famous scientist, or a movie star?

Hey, maybe if I click the camera, it will send me to a better time and place where I can be a queen or something. I totally do not want to be a hobo!

❈ *Turn to page 21.*

K it leads me into a dining room that is full of
people. It's as noisy and as full of life as Izza's
house. Everyone is sitting around a big table as if it's
an old-fashioned Thanksgiving, except they're eating
breakfast. Some of the people at the table are having
oatmeal *and* eggs *and* buttered toast *and* jelly *and* coffee. Mom and I don't eat this much for *dinner,* and our
breakfast is usually a power bar.

Buddy darts ahead and runs straight to a sleeping,
snoring brown-and-white basset hound.

"That's my dog, Grace," says Kit. "She sleeps a lot."

"She looks very sweet," I say.

Grace opens one eye, gives me a friendly look
and Buddy a friendly sniff, then goes back to sleep.
Buddy runs from person to person, wagging his tail
and demanding to be petted. Everyone smiles at him,
charmed. He *is* awfully appealing; he's just as sweet-
looking as Isabel's bunny Pippa, only in a lively,
perpetual-motion, wiggly puppy kind of way.
Naturally, everyone falls in love with him. I envy
Buddy. Meeting all these new people is harder for me.
I'm a lot less sure of how they'll react to me.

"Everyone, this is Lucille but she wants us to call

her Lulu," says Kit, "and this is her dog, Buddy."

Everyone looks up. "Hello, Lulu," they say. "Hey, Buddy!"

"Hello there, sweetheart!" says a sporty-looking man. "I'm Mr. Kittredge." He stands up and puts one arm around the shoulder of a slender, pretty woman, and with the other hand, he pats the shoulder of a teenage boy. He says, "This is Mrs. Kittredge, and our son, Charlie, who's home on leave from the CCC, and you've already met Kit. Welcome! We're glad you're here."

"Thanks," I say. I'm so self-conscious and awkward that my scalp feels sweaty and prickly. I don't know what to say. It doesn't help that Kit's brother is as handsome as a movie star! What does CCC stand for—Cool Cute Charlie? I've never had a brother, though, so maybe he'll turn out to be a Harry Sharma type of guy, who's good-looking but obnoxious.

Kit's mother looks like a movie star, too, in a pretty, old-fashioned, black-and-white-movie kind of way. She's wearing a fabulous bias-cut dress that I immediately think would look great on my mom. But her face is tired and worried looking.

"How do you do?" Kit's mom asks. When she

smiles, the tiredness falls away and she looks like Kit,
only grown up and without Kit's freckles. She gestures
to everyone at the table. "These are our boarders," she
says.

What's a *boarder*? These people are not snowboard-
ers or surfboarders, I can tell. But it's clear that they live
here, at the Kittredges' house, so I figure boarders must
be people who live in your house and maybe pay rent
or something.

Kit's mom introduces me to Mrs. Howard, who's
fluttery, and her son, Stirling, who's short and skinny.
Stirling says, "Hi." He has a surprisingly husky voice
for such a scrawny boy. Miss Hart and Miss Finney,
other boarders, are dressed in old-fashioned nurses'
uniforms, starched white hats and all! I notice that Kit's
mom doesn't tell me the grown-ups' first names. I can
tell that she expects me to use Mister, Missus, and Miss.

"Lulu is a great-niece of my Uncle Hendrick,"
explains Mrs. Kittredge. "Uncle Hendrick thought it
would be better—I mean, *pleasant* for us and more *fun*
for Lulu to stay with us for a while, instead of with
him." She turns to me. "Where is your suitcase, dear?"

"My—my suitcase?" I stammer. The boarders must

think I'm Clueless Lulu, a very, very dim bulb.

Kit says politely, "Lulu may not have been sure that she'd *want* to stay with us instead of Uncle Hendrick. After all, she doesn't know us. So she probably had her suitcase delivered to Uncle Hendrick's house from the train station."

"Instead of carrying it all the way up here," Stirling adds, "which was smart."

"Ah," says Mr. Kittredge. "Well, Lulu, if you want to stay with us—"

"Oh, I do!" I interrupt. Kit smiles at me.

"Good!" says Mr. Kittredge. "Then you and Kit can take the trolley down to Uncle Hendrick's house later and get your suitcase."

Why don't the Kittredges have a car? And who is this mysterious Uncle Hendrick, anyway? Everyone goes quiet whenever he's mentioned. I glance at Kit, but I can't tell what she is thinking. Her face has sort of shut down.

"Have you had your breakfast, Lulu?" Mrs. Kittredge asks. "I'd be glad to make you some oatmeal."

Oatmeal? Uh, no. I glance into the bowls on the table. Oatmeal is the stuff my mother uses to exfoliate when

she's giving herself a facial. "No, thank you,"
I say quickly. Everyone looks sort of surprised, as if
I'm crazy to turn down oatmeal.

"Then, if everyone will excuse me," says Mrs.
Kittredge, "I'll go prepare Lulu's room."

"I'll help you," says Mrs. Howard.

Now I must tell you that every person—except for
one—has obviously fallen in love with Buddy. The only
person who did not smile at Buddy was Mrs. Howard,
who seems a bit uptight, and for some odd reason,
Buddy immediately seems to have chosen her as his
special friend. Go figure! So when Mrs. Kittredge and
Mrs. Howard leave the room, so does Buddy.

Buddy follows his new love, Mrs. Howard, so
I follow him upstairs while everyone else finishes
breakfast. Mrs. Kittredge and Mrs. Howard go into
a big bedroom. I grab Buddy before he goes into the
bedroom. I don't mean to eavesdrop—really, I don't!—
but as I turn to carry Buddy downstairs, I can't help
overhearing when Mrs. Howard says, "Margaret, you
and Jack shouldn't give Lulu your room. Stirling and
I can move. You shouldn't be inconvenienced by
that spoiled young one, who turned up her nose at

oatmeal, and brought that annoying dog along."

Spoiled young one? Mrs. Howard means *me*. I hug Buddy for comfort. Clearly, I'm not wanted here.

Okay. This time-travel business has gone on long enough.

❦ *Turn to page 27.*

I put Buddy down. As I follow Kit through the front door, I glance behind me and see that he's carrying one end of a newspaper in his mouth. The newspaper is as big as he is, and he seems very proud of his ability to drag it. I give him a quick pat as I take the newspaper and set it on a small table in the hall. The headline is about President Franklin D. Roosevelt. *Say what?* Then I notice the date: September 1, 1933.

Whoa! That can't be right. I blink and read the date again, sure that I have goofed. Nope. There it is: 1933.

What on earth has happened to me? Where am I? What is going on? I'd say I was dreaming, but Buddy and Kit are totally real. Then it dawns on me: I have traveled back in time. When I clicked the camera, *bam!* I was transported back to 1933. Major weirdness, right?

How did it happen? Better question: How can I make it unhappen and go home? If the camera brought me here, will it take me home again? Do I dare try it?

❈ *To stay with Buddy and Kit,*
   turn to page 9.
❈ *To try the camera again,*
   turn to page 26.

I'm nervous and excited—but mostly curious—as I get ready to click the camera. Where will it take me? I close my eyes, click the camera, and . . .

Guess what? When I open my eyes, I'm back in my apartment.

Home.

Quiet.

Chilly.

Lonely.

Same old, same old.

I realize that Kit intrigues me. And at least when I'm Lulu in that parallel universe of the 1930s I have Buddy, right? A roly-poly puppy of my own. But hello—a *hobo*? Give me a break. Come on, camera—surely we can do better than that.

So, closing my eyes and holding my breath in suspense, I click the camera again.

❉ *Turn to page 22.*

Back in Kit's front yard, Buddy greets me, wriggling all over with delight. It seems that no time has passed. So that's how it works. The camera seems sure that I am meant to be with Kit. To tell the truth, I'm not really disappointed. Kit seems totally nice. And Buddy? Well, he's the dog I've always wanted.

Buddy and I walk around to the back of the house and across the backyard. Kit is waiting for us by a spigot next to the garage. There's a big vegetable garden, and I think I hear chickens, even though we seem to be in a city suburb, not the country.

"Nice garden," I say to Kit. Don't get me wrong—I am *not* a gardener. I never even water the potted plants Mom keeps on our balcony. But Camp Mosquito was all about stuff like composting and worms and growing your own vegetables.

Kit smiles at me. "Did you grow up on a farm?"

Of course, the truth is, I've never even *been* to a farm. So I say, "No, I'm really more of an indoors-y, city kind of person."

"Oh," says Kit kindly. "Did you work in a factory?"

Kids my age worked in factories in the 1930s? I thought there were laws about that kind of thing!

"Uh, no," I reply. "I was mostly a student."

Kit's face gets red, almost as if she's embarrassed for me. She whispers, "So your family was just like mine before the Depression. I know how it is. My dad lost his job a while ago. Now there's no money to send my brother Charlie to college, and we have to rent rooms in our house to boarders. We're scraping by, but it's hard to come up with twenty dollars for the mortgage every month, so we're always close to losing our house. Is that what happened to you?"

"Um, not exactly," I say. "My mother has a job. She's still at home. I, uh, left unexpectedly." That's an understatement!

"Ah, you ran away so that your family didn't have to feed you anymore," says Kit. "Last month, I met a teenage boy named Will. He's a hobo, and that's exactly what he did, too."

Man, this Depression sounds terrible! Imagine always being on the brink of losing your home, or running away so that your family doesn't have to feed you anymore. How sad is that? I can see why they call it a Depression.

Just then, Kit's mother appears carrying a plate of

sandwiches and a cloth sack. She nods toward the spigot. "Wash your face and hands, Lulu," she says. There's soap and a rough cloth next to the spigot, and I do as I'm told. Then Kit's mother hands me the plate and the sack and says, "I'm sorry we can't spare more."

"That's okay," I tell her. The sack is lumpy. I look inside and see that there are potatoes in it. I'm not sure what to do with them; I don't think potatoes can be eaten raw, can they? But I say, "Thank you very much."

"You are welcome, dear," says Kit's mom. She sighs again and smiles a sad smile as she leaves.

While I'm eating the sandwiches, Kit says, "I know Mother wishes she could do more to help you. But so many hoboes like you come up from the train. I guess the kind lady symbol must be on the fence again."

"The kind lady what?" I ask.

"You didn't see it?" asks Kit. She leads me around to the outside of the fence and points to a symbol chalked onto one of the boards. It looks like a cat.

"This is hobo code. It means that the lady who lives here is kindhearted and will give hoboes food as a handout or in return for doing chores." Kit looks at me very seriously. "You know, Lulu, if we could find some chores for you to do, Mother might let you and Buddy stay for a while."

❄ *To accept Kit's offer,
turn to page 28.*

❄ *To decline Kit's offer,
turn to page 83.*

I take a deep breath, close my eyes, click the camera, and . . . when I open my eyes I am home again, exactly, precisely where I was. I glance at the time on my laptop and see that it is exactly, precisely the moment it was before I left and found myself in 1933, with Kit.

My first thought is, *Phew! Glad I'm back.* That time travel was too weird!

Yeah, but it was pretty amazing, too. And no one missed me when I was gone. I'm curious about Kit and her family in 1933. Haven't I always wanted to see what was beyond the horizon? Isn't time travel a beyond-the-horizon adventure if there ever was one? And of course, I already miss that adorable puppy, Buddy, who's *my* dog in Kit's world.

Will the camera take me back to Kit's time so that I can be with Buddy and Kit again? Or will I land in another time, with other people?

I have to find out. I take a deep breath, close my eyes, and click the camera.

❈ *Turn to page 9.*

I'm just about to click the camera when I overhear Mrs. Kittredge reply, "I don't think Lulu is spoiled. I think she's just overwhelmed and shy."

"But giving up your room—" says Mrs. Howard.

"I'm giving it up gladly! To me, that girl is a wish come true," Mrs. Kittredge says. "Lulu has come just in the nick of time. We need her."

Say what? They *need* me? Or rather, they need Cousin Lucille. But why?

I bury my face in Buddy's fur and swallow hard. Suddenly I have a lump in my throat—not only because Mrs. Kittredge stuck up for me, but because even though I don't understand why, it's clear that the Kittredges are depending on me to help them in some way. This is a new sensation for me. No one's ever needed me before. I've certainly never had a whole family rely on me. And the Kittredges seem so nice; I don't want to let them down. Also, maybe most of all, I want Kit to be my friend.

I decide to stay and do whatever I can to help the Kittredges. Holding Buddy in my arms, I tiptoe silently downstairs.

❄ *Turn to page 31.*

hank you," I say slowly. "I would like to stay."
Kit looks really glad. She asks, "What chores
do you know how to do?"

Okay, now we've hit a snag. The only reason I even
know what chores *are* is because Laura and Mary did
them in the *Little House on the Prairie* books. Mom has
never taught me anything about housekeeping, and
our cleaning lady shoos me away if I offer to help her.
"Well," I say apologetically, "I'm afraid I don't know
how to do very much."

"I was just like you before Dad lost his job," Kit
says, looking at me with understanding. "I didn't know
anything about gardening, and I was hopeless at cooking and cleaning and doing the laundry until Mother
started the boardinghouse."

"Do you mind doing chores?" I ask Kit. I refrain
from pointing out that the word *chore* rhymes with *bore*.

Kit shrugs. "When we first started the boardinghouse, I resented chores. That's because before the Depression, I was used to doing just what I wanted to do
all day. But now . . . well, you know how it is, Lulu. I'm
sure the Depression changed how you feel about helping your family, too, didn't it? I mean, you ran away

from home to help your family save money."

I look down, ashamed. I've actually never done much of anything to help anybody, and I totally take for granted all that Mom does for me. But Kit is right: even knowing a little bit about the Depression has changed how I feel. *Note to self: Be more helpful from now on.* In fact, I'd like to begin by helping Kit right now. But I am at a loss as to how.

Kit seems to know that I feel awkward and useless. "We'll start with gardening," she says. "It'll be fun."

This I doubt. Gardens are home to all kinds of creepy-crawlies, so I'm not a big fan. At Camp Mosquito we had to touch disgusting slugs and gross worms and learn to identify poisonous snakes and tell the difference between an insect and an arachnid, which, really, who cares? They both *bug* me!

But I'm determined to help Kit, so I say, "Okay. You weed. I'll water." I figure that's safer, since all plants look like weeds to me and I'm likely to pull up a good one.

Kit hands me a gigantic watering can to fill at the spigot. I fill it and lug it back over to the garden. I'm getting sweaty, so I take off my coat and put it on a lawn chair.

"I love your coat," says Kit. "I've never seen one like it before."

I smile to myself, thinking that *no one* will see a coat like mine for another twenty years, since it's from the 1950s. But all I say is, "Thanks. It's not fashionable right now, but I like it too." As I pour water on the plants, I ask, "Do you grow all the vegetables that you eat?"

"Most of them," says Kit. "We used to have only flowers. But you can't eat flowers, so we dug them out and planted vegetables instead. Lots of people grow food now to save money. We keep chickens, too, behind the garage!"

So I *did* hear chickens. "It's like a little farm!" I say.

Kit laughs, and then sings, *"Kit and Lulu have a farm, ee-I, ee-I, oh!"*

And I chime in with: *"And on our farm we have some chickens, ee-I, ee-I, eeeeeek!"* I shriek. "Kit—watch out! Snake, *snake*!"

❄ *Turn to page 34.*

When I get downstairs, no one is in the dining room except for Kit, who is gathering the breakfast dishes from the table, and Grace, who is still asleep. I don't know what else to do, so I put Buddy down and start clearing dishes too, like Kit. There sure are a lot of dishes.

"Excuse me, Lulu," says Kit. "But you shouldn't help me. You're a guest."

"I want to help," I say. "I can share your chores. And would it be okay if I share your room, too?"

Kit shakes her head. "That's nice of you, Lulu," she says slowly. "But if you share my chores and my room, Uncle Hendrick might not . . ." She stops.

"Might not what?"

Kit blushes. "Uncle Hendrick is giving us money to have you stay here. You are a paying guest. A boarder. And we—well, we really need the money."

Okay, so *that's* what they need me for: money. Money is something I have never had to worry about, because of Mom's job. But Kit and her mother have both made it clear they *really* need that money from Uncle Hendrick. I feel a little strange about being needed for money. "Kit," I say, "I hate to be nosy, but why does

your family need money so badly?"

Kit sighs. "My dad lost his job," she says, "because of the Depression."

"Your dad lost his job because he's depressed?" I ask. "You mean he got fired because he was sad?"

"No," says Kit. "The Depression. You know, how people got nervous about their money and so they stopped buying things, and then even more people lost their jobs. I'm sure the city where you live has been affected by the Depression, too. My dad used to sell cars, but people stopped buying cars because they didn't have enough money. Dad kept hoping things would get better. He tried to keep his car dealership open, and even paid his workers out of his own savings. But eventually, he ran out of money and had to close the car dealership. So my mother had the idea of taking boarders into our house. We depend on their rent money to pay the mortgage, which is twenty dollars a month that we owe to the bank. The rent money also goes to buy food and to pay our bills and, well, for *everything.*"

Now I understand why Mrs. Kittredge said that I was a "wish come true."

Kit squares her shoulders and says sort of fiercely,

"Uncle Hendrick thinks that the boardinghouse is a bad idea, but I'm proud of us for trying to make it work, even though I have to admit that sometimes I don't like living in such a crowded house, always full of people."

"And now here *I* am. *Another* person in your house. And Buddy, too."

"Oh, I would *like* having you and Buddy as boarders," says Kit. "I'd like it a lot. I'd be really sorry if Uncle Hendrick wouldn't let you stay here because we weren't treating you as a guest."

❆ *To do as Kit asks and act as a guest,*
turn to page 36.

❆ *To insist on sharing Kit's chores and room,*
turn to page 42.

My worst nightmare, and it's happening for real. There's a big brown snake—I can tell it's a copperhead, which is very venomous—coiled and ready to strike Kit, who is kneeling in the dirt under the potato plants. "It's a copperhead!" I shout.

Without asking any questions, Kit scoops up Buddy. I grab her from behind and yank with all my strength to pull her away from the snake. Kit and Buddy topple back on top of me and we all fall down in a tangled tumble of legs and arms and paws onto the grass. Out of the corner of my eye, I see the copperhead slither away.

Kit and I sit on the grass, panting. I hug Buddy, feeling shaky and shuddery and a little sick to my stomach.

"Gosh," breathes Kit.

"You can say that again," I gasp.

"How did you know that was a copperhead?" Kit asks.

I manage a wobbly grin. "My mom made me go to a science camp. I did *not* like it, because I'm deathly afraid of snakes. But now I'm glad she made me go."

"Your camp sounds like one of the free programs for children that we have here in our parks here, too,"

says Kit. "I'm glad you went. You saved my life."

"And Buddy's life, too," says Kit's mother, striding toward us. "I saw it all from the house. You're a brave girl, Lulu."

"You know what I think you should do?" Kit says to me. "Write a letter to your mother. Tell her that you're safe. And tell her that now you're *glad* she sent you to camp because you saved Buddy and me from a poisonous snake."

"Speaking as a mother," says Mrs. Kittredge, "I think Kit's idea is splendid." She smiles and goes back inside.

Kit tilts her head at me. "So how about it? Do you want to go write that letter to your mother?"

❈ To go inside to write a letter,
    turn to page 38.

❈ To stay outside and avoid writing,
    turn to page 48.

Okay," I tell Kit. "I'll stay in your parents' room, and I won't try to do any chores. I'm totally hopeless at housework anyway."

Kit smiles and looks relieved. "I think that'll be for the best, Lulu."

"Well, except I *will* bring these plates into the kitchen," I say, gesturing with the stack of plates in my hands. "I can handle this much, at least. And what Uncle Hendrick doesn't know won't hurt him."

Kit grins. "All right!"

The dogs and I follow Kit into the kitchen. I set the dishes on the counter and then sit, awkwardly and uselessly, and watch as Kit washes the breakfast dishes. When she has dried the last dish and wiped the counter, she says, "Now it's time to do the laundry."

We go to the basement, where Kit starts to stuff dirty clothes into a gigantic machine that looks like The Monster That Ate Antarctica. I mean, you have never seen a washing machine as big and ungainly as this thing! It stands on bowlegged legs and has big wooden rollers on top. I watch quietly as Kit puts shirts, socks, aprons, underwear, and pajamas into it. But as she's about to stuff in a wool sweater, I gasp, "Don't do that!"

"Don't do what?" Kit looks puzzled and startled.

"Don't put that sweater in the washer. It's made of wool," I explain. "If you put wool in the clothes washer, it'll be ruined."

"How do you know?" Kit asks.

"Well, um, clothes and fabrics are sort of my hobby." I don't mention that at home, in my own time, lots of the old, vintage clothes I find at secondhand stores are made of wool. "Trust me, I've learned the hard way that wool stuff can't be tossed in the washer. When wool gets all twisted and mangled, it shrinks."

"I've been doing the laundry for a while now," Kit admits, "but I'm still not very good at it." She grins and says, "Thanks!"

I smile back. "You're welcome. Here, I'll show you how to wash that sweater by hand, in cold, soapy water."

We go back up to the kitchen to wash the sweater in the sink. Kit and I get really wet and soapy ourselves, and the floor gets so wet and soapy that we end up mopping it. But it's fun, and I can tell that Kit appreciates that I stopped her from wrecking her sweater.

❈ *Turn to page 51.*

Okay," I tell Kit. "Sure, why not."

"Then let's go," Kit says.

I pick up my coat and the sack of potatoes, and with Buddy leaping joyfully at our feet, Kit and I run inside the house and up two flights of stairs to Kit's room, which turns out to be in the attic.

A sleepy-looking basset hound greets us at the top of the stairs. "Hi, Grace," says Kit, gently stroking one of Grace's long, droopy ears. Buddy bounces all around Grace, who smiles a drooly smile at him, and they are instant friends.

At home, I'd toss my coat and the sack of potatoes on the floor and they'd sink into the mess like a rock in the ocean. But Kit's room is organized and orderly, so I'm careful to put my coat and the sack on a chair. There are four alcoves with windows. One alcove has a bed and a big plant. In another there's a comfy-looking chair, a lamp, and a bookshelf overloaded with enticing books. In the third alcove there's a baseball glove and bat and a tennis racket and balls, and in the last alcove there's a big desk with a typewriter on it.

"Your room is adorable," I tell Kit. "It reminds me of Sara Crewe's attic in *A Little Princess*."

"Oh, have you read that book, too?" Kit asks.

"Yes! It's one of my favorites."

"My friend Ruthie and I like it, too," says Kit. She looks around her room and grins a little. "Just like Sara Crewe, I was sad when I first moved up here. I had to give up my bedroom downstairs so we could rent it to boarders. But then I set up this attic room exactly the way I wanted it, and now I love it."

"I do, too," I say, thinking how cool it is that Kit flipped a bummer into something good. I wonder if I could do that? I mean, change what bugs me instead of moping and complaining about it.

Kit points to a black typewriter on the desk. "My dad fixed up this typewriter for me because I love to write, and I'm hoping to be a reporter when I grow up. You can use it to type a letter to your mother. I'll be in the garden." She leaves, and Buddy goes with her.

I've never touched a typewriter before. Boy, you have to push those keys down hard! And guess what? There's no exclamation point on the keyboard. After experimenting, I discover I can make one by typing an apostrophe, then hitting backspace and putting a period under it. You can't delete misspelled words, and

there's no spell check, and I am not quite a spelling bee
champion—so the letter is kind of polka-dotted with
words I cross out and retype until they look sort of cor-
rect. Anyway, I finally manage to type out this letter:

Dear Mom,

I hope you're sitting down, because
you're going to be ~~surprized~~ surprised
when you read this: THANK YOU FOR SENDING
ME TO SCIENCE CAMP!

Yes, you read it correctly. Even though
I was grumpy about Camp ~~Musqueete~~
Mosquitoh, now I am ~~greatful~~ gratefull
that I went. I was helping a friend of
mine in her garden, and because of what
I learned at camp, I was able to save her
and a dog from being bitten by a ~~poisenus~~
poisonous snake! I never expected that
anything I learned at camp would be useful, but knowing about snakes saved my
friend's--and the dog's--life! Mom, if I
had a dog, I promise I would be ~~rispen~~
responsible for it. I know that I can be a

good pet owner. I proved it to myself when
I saved the dog's life today.

Please, after you read this, can we
talk about getting a dog?

Love,

Your from-grumpy-to-grateful daughter,

Me

❈ *Turn to page 44.*

In that case," I say, "if I ever see Uncle Hendrick, I'll tell him that I *made* you let me help you with your chores. I promise." Remembering what Mrs. Howard called me, I add, "And you can tell Uncle Hendrick that I'm a 'spoiled young one' and I'm used to having my own way, and I absolutely *insisted* that you let me share your room."

Kit smiles but looks doubtful. If she doubts that I will be of much help with chores, she's right. Mom has a housekeeper clean our apartment, so I don't really know much about dusting or housework. I'll be especially useless in this 1930s house with its weird or nonexistent appliances! I think they have electricity, but I haven't seen a computer or a TV anywhere.

Finally, Kit shrugs and says, "Okay. We'll give it a try."

We collect stacks of dishes and carry them in, Buddy scampering around our feet. Kit uses her elbow to open a swinging door, and Grace leads us into what must be the kitchen. It has a sink that looks like a tub, and a stove that looks like a Mars landing vehicle. There's no microwave, no blender, no food processor, not even a toaster oven. I look around. "Where's the dishwasher?"

"*I'm* the dishwasher," Kit says. "We don't have money for a maid, especially since . . ." She bites her lip. Then she says, "Mother and I do all the housework."

"Well, I'll help. It'll be fun, and you'll be finished faster." I've never actually washed dishes by hand before, but how hard can it be?

"Okay," says Kit. She turns on the hot water and nods toward a box next to the sink. "Sprinkle some soap into the water."

"Okay!" I say. I turn the box and shake it, and soap flakes come cascading out in a blizzard.

"Whoa!" says Kit. But it's too late. The sink begins overflowing with bubbles. They float up into the air, spill over the sink onto the floor, and burble out onto the counters next to the sink. Buddy barks with delight and Grace howls as Kit and I try to bat the bubbles back, but soon our arms and chests are coated with bubbles, too.

"I'm sorry!" I say. "Oh, Kit, I'm so sorry!"

❧ *Turn to page 46.*

A fter I finish typing my letter, it occurs to me that I have to deliver it in person. If I really want a dog, and I do, then I have to put the letter in my pocket, click the camera, and go home and give the letter to Mom. I realize I'll be very, very sorry to leave Kit and Buddy; I feel a pang in my heart just thinking of how much I will miss them, but in spite of that, I know that it's time for me to go.

I'm sort of excited about going home as I fold my letter and put it in my pocket. Then I scribble a note:

Dear Kit,

Thank you for teaching me to be helpful and to appreciate what I have. Right now, what I have is a heart that's happy and miserable at the same time. It's telling me to go home. I will never forget you.

Love,

Lulu

P.S. I know that you and Grace will take good care of Buddy.

P.P.S. The coat is for you.

I pin the note to the coat, tickled at the idea of how fashion-forward Kit will look when she wears it. Then,

before I can change my mind, I click the camera.

Back home in my room, remembering how organized and inviting Kit's room was, I straighten things up and put away all the stuff that's lying on the floor. Then I go out onto the balcony and stare at the horizon as if I could see past it to Kit.

The moon is very bright. It shines on the plants that Mom has lined up in a hopeful parade. They look thirsty and slightly wilted, so I fill the watering can and give each plant a healthy drink. I'm pulling off dead leaves, thinking about how Kit and I worked together in her garden, when Mom comes out.

"Hey, thanks for taking care of the plants," she says. "And you tidied your room, too."

"You're welcome," I say. "I got the idea of helping from a friend of mine. She gave me the idea of writing *this*, too." I pull the letter I typed out of my pocket and hand it to Mom. "It's for you."

❀ *The End* ❀

To read this story another way and see how different choices lead to a different ending, turn back to page 25.

Much to my surprise, Kit starts to laugh. In fact, she laughs so hard that she practically collapses into the gigantic sink. "I know I shouldn't laugh," she gasps, "because it's bad to waste the soap. But you look so funny! You have a cap of bubbles on your head. You look like a snowman!"

Immediately, I make myself a beard of bubbles. "Ho, ho, ho. I'm Santa Claus." I put a blob of bubbles on Buddy's head and Grace's, too. "Buddy and Grace are elves."

Kit holds up a tall mound of bubbles. "I'm the Statue of Liberty," she says.

Kit and I burst out singing together: "*My country 'tis of thee, sweet land of liberty, of thee I sing . . .*" Then Kit turns on the radio and we listen to jazzy songs that I figure are the hit tunes of 1933. Kit scrubs the dishes in the (very) soapy water and rinses them. I dry.

After we finish the dishes, we don't waste the soapy water. We use it to wipe off the counters and mop up the floor. Kit tells me, "My Aunt Millie always says, 'Use it up, wear it out, make it do, or do without.' She'd say that even soapy water shouldn't be wasted."

I nudge Kit and tilt my head toward Buddy. "My

dog's not wasting the wet floor, either," I say. Kit and I laugh as Buddy skitters and skates across the wet floor and bumps into Grace, who doesn't seem to mind.

❈ *Turn to page 51.*

Gosh, Kit—I'm not much of a writer," I tell her. "Anyway, if I stay out here with you and Buddy, the work will go faster."

"Well, okay," says Kit. She grins. "I've got to admit that I'm glad for your help."

It's hot in the garden. The sun burns down mercilessly, and soon Kit and I are both sweaty. There's dirt smeared on my pants, and my shoes are wet from the watering can. Kit has dirt on her face and hands, and her sundress has a blob of mud on it.

So wouldn't you know, just as we stand up, some boy screeches to a stop on his bike and stares at us over the garden fence. "Well, if it isn't Kit Kittredge," the boy says.

"Hello, Roger," says Kit warily.

"I knew you were a maid since your dad lost his job," sneers Roger. "And now I see that you're a dirt farmer, too."

Kit's eyes meet mine. By silent agreement, we both studiously ignore Roger so he'll give up and go away. But it doesn't work.

"School's starting up again pretty soon," Roger goes on. "You'd better begin scrubbing the dirt off your

hands now. And look at your clothes! You look like a scarecrow! That's probably your back-to-school outfit, since your dad can't afford to buy you anything new to wear. Or maybe you'll get lucky and get a dress made out of a flour sack."

Jerk alert, right? Even obnoxious Harry Sharma has never said anything so nasty to me! So I turn and say, "Hey Roger, guess what?"

"What?" says Roger.

"Knock, knock."

"What?" says Roger again. First I think: This dude makes Harry Sharma look like Albert Einstein, brain-wise! Then I realize that knock-knock jokes probably haven't been invented yet, so I do the whole thing myself, saying:

"Knock, knock.

Who's there?

Roger.

Roger who?

Roger, over and out."

"Hunh?" bleats Roger.

"Oh, come on, Roger," I say. "You can figure it out. Let's try it again. Knock, knock."

"Uh, who's there?" asks Roger.

"Boo," I say.

Roger says, "Boo who?"

"Boo hoo?" I repeat. "Don't be such a crybaby, Roger. It's just a joke!"

Kit bursts out laughing. Roger gets all red in the face and mutters, "Ha, ha. Very funny."

Meanwhile, Buddy discovers the chickens and barks at them through the chicken wire, setting off a perfect storm of wild cackling and clucking and wing flapping and chaotic chicken sounds from inside the coop mixed with howls from Grace, who joins in from inside the house. The timing is perfect—it sounds as if the dogs and the chickens are laughing at Roger. This just does him in, and he pedals off in a huff.

"*Roger, over and out!*" Kit shouts after him.

"*Very* over and *very* out," I add, for good measure.

Then we both holler as loud as we can, "*Boo hoo, boo hoo!*"

We grab Buddy so that the hens will calm down, and collapse against each other, laughing.

❋ *Turn to page 52.*

J ust then, Mrs. Kittredge comes into the kitchen. She raises her eyebrows when she sees how wet Kit and I are, but she smiles when she sees the washed dishes and freshly scrubbed kitchen counters and mopped floor. "Why, thank you, Kit," she says.

"Lulu helped me," Kit says generously.

"Kit didn't want me to help, but I insisted," I add quickly.

"Ah, so that's why you're both wet," says Mrs. Kittredge. "Lulu, you need dry clothes."

"We'll go to Uncle Hendrick's house now and pick up her suitcase," says Kit.

"Good idea," says Mrs. Kittredge, giving us another smile as she leaves the room.

Yikes! I do not want to go to Uncle Hendrick's. If Uncle Hendrick has ever met this Lucille person, he'll know I'm not her—and then what will I tell everyone?

❀ *To avoid going to Uncle Hendrick's house, turn to page 58.*

❀ *To go with Kit to Uncle Hendrick's house, turn to page 94.*

When Roger has completely disappeared, Kit and I wash off at the spigot as well as we can. Our hands and faces are clean, but Kit's sundress and my pants are wet and streaked with mud. As we go inside, I notice that Kit seems a little down.

"What's the matter?" I ask. "You're not bothered by that creep, are you? Don't let old Rotten Roger get to you, Kit. I know doorknobs that are smarter than Roger."

"Roger is rotten," says Kit, "but I'm afraid that he's right about my clothes." She holds out the skirt of her wrinkled and muddy sundress and makes a face. "Even when this dress is clean, it's still old and faded. I have one really nice red dress, but it's too good to wear to school. I have to save it for church and parties. I wish . . ."

She stops.

"You wish what?" I ask.

"I wish I could have a new dress to wear on the first day of school," Kit says, in a whispery rush, as if she is ashamed. "But I know it's not possible. There's no money for a new dress. If we did have any extra money, we'd put it toward sending Charlie to

college. But as it is, my parents need every penny. The mortgage is a lot—twenty dollars a month."

Now I feel a little down, too. I mean, Izza and I blow twenty dollars just going to the movies! I wish I had a twenty-dollar bill—and a new outfit—to give Kit right now.

Kit opens the door and we step into the kitchen, where six people all look at me with curiosity.

A nice-looking man says, "You must be Lulu. My wife told me about you. I'm Kit's father." He tilts his head toward a tall teenage boy and a short younger boy who are sitting at the table making a kite and says with a smile, "This is Kit's brother, Charlie, and one of our boarders, Stirling Howard."

"Hi, Lulu," say the boys.

"Hi," I say, blushing and inwardly kicking myself for the fact that I'm meeting all these people while looking like a wreck. Charlie is movie-star handsome, I'm not kidding.

Mrs. Kittredge says, "And these are more of our boarders. This is Stirling's mother, Mrs. Howard, and Miss Hart and Miss Finney."

All three ladies say, "How do you do, Lulu?" all at

once, which sounds so comical that we all start laughing, so I feel comfortable right away. For a second I think that Miss Hart and Miss Finney must be on their way to a costume party because they are decked out in old-fashioned nurses' uniforms with white stockings, white shoes, starched white dresses, and stiff white hats that perch on their heads like doves. Then I realize that in the 1930s, that's how nurses actually dressed.

Mrs. Kittredge says, "Lulu, thank you for helping Kit in the garden. We'll be having lunch in a while. Won't you stay?"

"That's really nice of you," I reply, "but I think I should go." Mrs. Kittredge has been gracious, but I'm aware that she'd have to stretch the food she has even farther to give me lunch. The Kittredges are growing food in order to save money. I don't want to be an expense to them.

As I pick up the potato sack to leave, Kit looks stricken. She says, "I'll walk you to the train yard, Lulu."

"Oh," says Mrs. Kittredge, "that reminds me. Kit, I put a box of old clothes in your bedroom. Would you take it with you and drop it off at a soup kitchen or a

church on your way to the train yard with Lulu?"

"Sure," says Kit. "Come on, Lulu."

I go upstairs with Kit. Her attic room is quirky and fun looking, with four alcoves tucked under a steep roof. Every alcove is decorated differently: one has a desk, one has a soft-looking reading chair, one has a bed, and one has sports equipment. But I hardly notice the room, because when I spot the box of Mrs. Kittredge's old clothes, my eyes pop out of my head.

Oh my *gosh*. I lift one dress out of the box and practically *flip out* because it is so gorgeous. The material Mrs. Kittredge's old dress is made out of is to die for. It's a wonderful, slippery, featherweight cotton sateen that catches the light as if it were silk. I love the rosy color of the background, and the bright, cheery flowers scattered in bunches all over it. There's a coffee stain on the skirt near the hem, the lacy collar is unraveled, and one of the sleeves is frayed beyond repair, so I can see why Mrs. Kittredge thinks it is unusable. But my heart is beating fast, and I am so excited that I can hardly breathe.

"Kit," I burble, "your mother is giving this dress away, right? So she doesn't want it anymore, right? So

she wouldn't mind if I, like, changed it, right?"

"Uh, right, I guess," says Kit, sounding a little confused.

"Okay, then, we're in business." I turn Kit so that she has her back to the mirror. "Put your arms up, stand still, and prepare to be amazed." Before Kit can make a peep of protest, I slip the dress over her head. "This," I say dramatically, "is going to be the most spectacular back-to-school dress ever."

"But—" Kit begins.

"Trust me." Kit looks puzzled, so I explain, "Clothes are my hobby. I like to mess around with them, taking old clothes apart and putting them back together in different ways to make new outfits. I know it's sort of a silly thing to do, but—"

"Silly?" says Kit. "Mother is always trying to make over our old clothes to get more wear out of them. But this dress is hopeless, isn't it?"

"Not to me!" I say.

Kit fetches a pair of scissors and a sewing basket from her mother's room. I kneel at Kit's feet and take a deep breath. Mom always says that I'm fearless with scissors, but I'm sort of nervous now, because I've never

altered a dress for anyone else before, only for myself. And this dress has to be perfect. *This* dress is for my friend—Kit.

Snip, snip, snip. I cut a swath that includes the coffee stain off the hem to make the dress short enough for Kit. I pull off the tattered lace collar and remove the sleeves. Now that I've begun, I don't feel nervous anymore—I feel excited as I cut, snip, pin, and baste. I don't have time to sew the seams or the hem carefully. That will have to be done later. But I cut the collar off a white shirt and tack that onto the neckline, and *presto, change-o*, a pretty dress has taken shape.

"There!" I turn Kit around so that she is facing the mirror. "What do you think?"

"Gosh, Lulu," gasps Kit, astounded. She bounces on her toes. "Oh, I love it. I love it! However did you make something so pretty out of Mother's old dress?"

I shrug, even though really, I've never felt so proud in my life. Who'd have guessed that my goofy hobby would turn out to be so useful?

❉ *Turn to page 61.*

I realize it will look weird if I walk around in my coat while I wait for my clothes to dry. If only the Kittredges had a dryer, I could put my clothes in it and borrow a bathrobe or something while my clothes dried. But dryers haven't been invented yet, or if they have, the Kittredges don't have one, which means that I have a problem.

I gather up my courage and tell Kit the truth. "Kit," I say, "there's no reason to go to Uncle Hendrick's house to get my clothes. My suitcase isn't there."

"It's not?"

I don't want to lie to Kit. I rack my brain. "My suitcase was left behind," I say finally. This is sort of true. Back in my apartment, I *do* have that suitcase full of old clothes I'm planning to redo, and I *was* looking at the suitcase before I clicked the camera, and the suitcase *was* left behind.

"That's too bad," Kit says kindly. "Well, never mind. Come upstairs with me to my room. You can borrow some of my clothes."

We go upstairs, Buddy taking the lead. I love the way he is always so enthusiastic, bounding ahead or following us without a leash. Grace brings up the rear.

I've never seen a calmer dog. She moves in slow-mo.

"Wow!" I say. Kit's room is the attic, so the ceiling is high in the middle and slants all the way to the floor on the sides, with windows tucked in alcoves. "I love your room, Kit."

Kit beams proudly. "I love it, too, though I didn't at first. I had to give up my regular room to Mrs. Howard and Stirling. But then I realized that I could decorate however I wanted to up here. No one cared. So I had this brainstorm. To turn the attic into a bedroom, *my* bedroom, I used every alcove differently."

"You sure did make the best of it!" In fact, Kit has done the neatest thing. One alcove has sports stuff, one has a desk and typewriter, one has a bed and a plant, and one has a big reading chair, which Buddy jumps into, and a bookshelf heavy with books. And Kit's room is neat in the sense of *tidy*, too. It makes me ashamed of my messy room at home. Mom always says it looks like a cyclone hit a combination library and sporting-goods store, and that's why I can never find anything. Shoes, tennis balls, towels, T-shirts, books from school, books about dogs, clothing redesign projects I never finished, soccer cleats, library books, sometimes a bowl that has

dried-up cereal in it, socks, wires for my laptop—the list can go on and on when it comes to the stuff and junk that's piled up in my room. So, yeah, I guess Mom has a point. Maybe when I go back to the twenty-first century, I'll try to make the best of my room, too, and take some pride in it, as Kit does in hers. I could keep it tidier, for starters.

❀ *Turn to page 63.*

ome on!" says Kit. She grabs me by the hand
and drags me behind her as she runs downstairs and outside to the backyard. Mrs. Howard and
Mrs. Kittredge are hanging clothes on the clothesline,
Mr. Kittredge is digging potato plants, and Charlie and
Stirling are weeding with the dubious help of Buddy
and Grace. It's late afternoon, and the yard is washed in
a sunny, golden glow.

"Look, everybody!" Kit says. "Look at the gorgeous
dress Lulu made for me!" She twirls around so that the
skirt swirls, and everybody oohs and ahhs and claps.

Mr. Kittredge sweeps Kit up in a wild waltz around
the yard, and everyone starts talking at once.

"Could that possibly be my old dress?" gasps Mrs.
Kittredge.

"Lulu, you are a genius," says Charlie.

"My word, that dress is dreamy," says Mrs. Howard.

"It's a movie star's dress!" says Mr. Kittredge. "Kit,
sweetie, you look like a million bucks!"

Kit and her dad waltz over to me and Kit says,
"Thank you, Lulu! Thank you, thank you, thank you.
Now I cannot *wait* to go back to school."

I laugh. "Watch out, Roger!" But believe it or not,

weirdly, I feel grateful to Roger. He didn't mean to, but he revealed something that Kit was longing for—and something that I could give her.

We're all talking and laughing so much that at first, we don't hear the big, black, purring car drive up, or the little girl jump out of it and shout happily, "Scooter! Oh, Scooter!" She rushes over and falls to her knees to hug Buddy, who rises up on his back legs so that he can lick her face all over in spasms of love and joy.

"Buddy?" I say softly.

The little girl's father says, "Hi, hello there, folks! Sorry to barge in like this. Ann and I are just so thrilled to find her puppy, Scooter, you'll have to excuse us!"

"I beg your pardon?" says Mr. Kittredge. "You say Buddy—I mean, you say this is *your* little girl's dog?"

"Yes," says the man, who's wearing an expensive-looking suit. "We've been searching for Scooter all day. We've looked from one end of Cincinnati to the other; I knew Ann would never give up until she'd found him."

Mr. Kittredge turns to me. "Lulu, I thought Buddy was *your* dog."

✖ *Turn to page 66.*

K it opens her closet and holds out an adorable red dress. They really knew fashion and style in the 1930s! The dress has a wonderful, wide white collar with an asymmetrical point, and the skirt is sort of shaped like a bell. "Here," Kit says. "You can wear this."

"Oh," I sigh. I love the dress! But clearly, this is her very best dress. I can't borrow it. If I wear it back to the twenty-first century, Kit will lose it. And let's face it: I'm sloppy. The dress's wide white collar has "spill catcher" written all over it. I'd be mortified if I ruined Kit's best dress. While I'm wondering what to say, I spot a box of clothes next to Grace, near the chair that Buddy's in. "What are those?" I ask.

"They're old clothes I've outgrown," says Kit.

"Old clothes?" I say. I begin to look at the clothes in the box, holding them up to inspect them. Some of them are *fabulous* vintage materials. I mean, if I saw these in a secondhand store, I would *flip*. I see potential right away. I pull out a pair of jean overalls. "I'll wear these."

But Kit shakes her head. "I can't let you wear my old clothes. Mother wouldn't like it. And if Uncle Hendrick

were to see you in them, I'm afraid he'd—"

"Freak out? I mean, get mad at you?"

Kit nods. I can tell Kit is a girl who has a lot of pride, the *good* kind of pride, not the stuck-up kind. And it would hurt her pride to have Uncle Hendrick scold her.

"Listen, Kit," I say. "Your dress is nice. Actually, it's *too* nice. I just need something to throw on while my clothes dry."

"Okay," she says with a shrug. A grin spreads over her face as she watches me concoct an outfit for myself out of her old clothes. I fold up the frayed cuffs of a blouse, twist the straps of the denim overalls so that they fit me, use a scarf as a belt, and *ta-da!* Fabulous, if I do say so myself.

"Gosh," says Kit. "How'd you do that?"

"Oh," I say breezily, "making old clothes look new is my idea of fun." I point to the alcoves and say, "You had fun using old stuff in new ways when you fixed up your room, right? It's the same thing, really."

"I guess it is," Kit laughs. "And you're sure you don't mind wearing those clothes while you wait for your suitcase to get here?"

"Not at all." I *don't* add, "Which is a good thing, because we may be waiting for that suitcase forever."

"I've been meaning to take the old clothes in that box to a soup kitchen and give them away," says Kit. "Do you want to come do that with me?"

Give them away? My hands are, like, *itching* to work with the clothes in the box. I know I could make some terrific outfits for Kit and me. Then it hits me like a ton of bricks: here Kit's family is struggling, yet she still wants to help people who are worse off than she is.

I swallow hard. No one will ever know how much of a sacrifice I'm making as I pick up the box and I say, "Absolutely. Let's go."

❈ *Turn to page 68.*

No," I say miserably. "I never knew where he came from. But I loved him so much, I wanted him to be mine." Everyone can see that I am close to tears, and they are all too nice to ask me any more questions.

"Oh, I am sorry," says Ann's father, very kindly. "Here." He thrusts a twenty-dollar bill into my hands. "We offered a reward for Scooter's safe return. Ann has been heartbroken and sick with worry about him. Thank you so much for taking good care of Scooter today. I don't know what we would have done if anything had happened to him. Ann loves him so."

Mrs. Kittredge stands behind me and puts her hands on my shoulders to comfort me. "He's a very lovable dog," she says. "We're glad he's back with his own family again."

I'm fighting back tears, even though I know that this is for the best. Buddy can't come back to the twenty-first century with me, and it is clear that he loves Ann and she loves him. I pick Buddy up, give him one last hug, and hand him to Ann.

She says shyly, "We live not too far from here. You can visit any time you want."

"And we're taking a trip next month," Ann's father says. "We'll need someone to look after Scooter while we're away. I'd pay you, of course."

"Oh, we'd be glad to look after your dog!" says Kit.

"Splendid," says Ann's father.

Then we all wave good-bye as Ann and her father leave, driving away in their luxurious-looking car, taking Buddy with them.

Suddenly, I turn around and run inside.

❄ *Turn to page 73.*

S tirling and my friend Ruthie and I have been to this soup kitchen before," says Kit as we walk along with the box of old clothes. "So I know Mrs. Schultz, the lady in charge."

We turn the corner onto River Street. "Whoa," I breathe when I see the line outside the soup kitchen. "I didn't expect to see so many people." The line is four people across and stretches from the door of the soup kitchen all the way down the block. By now it is nearly midday, and the sun is beating down. There's no shade, and the people waiting in line in the fierce summer sunshine look hot, thirsty, dirty, tired, and miserable. "There are whole families here," I add. "Even families with little babies."

I mean, I know there are homeless families in my time, too, but I guess I've just never seen them lined up for free food. And these children are in rags. Their clothes are ripped and filthy, held together by a thread. Their shoes (if they have any at all—many are barefoot) are worse than their clothes. Some have sacks tied around their feet. Some have shoes that are much too big, or clearly too small. I pick up Buddy and give him a hug.

"It's sad, isn't it?" says Kit.

Kit has this way of saying exactly what I'm think-ing. So I just nod.

It is hot inside the soup kitchen, and the aroma of soup and coffee is so strong you could swim in it. The room is full of tables, and every table is crowded with people eating bread and soup and drinking coffee. The food is served at a long table in a setup that reminds me of the cafeteria line at school—except that everyone in the line is polite and patient.

"Excuse me, Mrs. Schultz," Kit says to the woman in charge. "We've brought some clothes to give away. They're children's clothes."

"Bless you!" says Mrs. Schultz. The frames of her eyeglasses are perfectly round, so she looks like a wise, kindly owl. "The children need clothes desperately." She smiles at Buddy, who wags not only his tail but his whole body with joy, and adds, "They need fun, too, so I'm glad you brought your dog along. So many of them had to leave behind the pets they loved." Mrs. Schultz gestures toward a group of four girls sitting on the floor in a corner, talking quietly. "Please give the clothes to those girls. Their family lost everything in a fire."

"Yes, ma'am," says Kit.

Suddenly, I feel really awkward. I've never spoken to a homeless person before. I grab Kit's sleeve and whisper, "Won't the girls think we're snooty snobs who're giving them clothes that we think are good enough for *them* but not good enough for *us*?"

"No," says Kit. "Trust me."

Kit sits right down on the floor with the girls and smiles. "Hi," she says in an easy, friendly, comfortable way. "My friend and I brought some clothes." She takes a blue shirt out of the box and offers it to the girl next to her. "I think this will fit you."

Taking my cue from Kit's friendliness, I pipe up, "The blue will bring out the pretty blue of your eyes."

"Thanks," says the girl quietly. She seems shy, until Buddy bounces onto her lap and practically knocks her over by licking her chin. That makes everyone laugh, and suddenly we all feel comfortable.

Without making a big, show-offy deal about it, Kit hands out the clothes to the girls. And it turns out that I'm a whiz at eyeballing sizes and finding something in the box that will fit each girl just right. The older girls say thank you, and the younger ones just smile shyly,

but they all look pumped. As Izza would say, it's all good.

When we have handed out all the clothes, Kit and I say good-bye to the girls and then find Mrs. Schultz so that we can say good-bye to her, too.

"Thank you for giving the girls those clothes," says Mrs. Schultz, "and thank you even more for giving them a reason to laugh." She stoops down and scratches Buddy on the head. "You are a miracle worker," she says to Buddy, who looks up at her with adoring puppy eyes. "I wish you could come here every day and work your magic on these children. Heaven knows they need the sort of happiness that a darling dog like you can bring."

We say good-bye, and as we head to the door, Kit sighs. "When I see the people here, it makes me appreciate my family," she says. "We may be pinching pennies, and our house is crowded and noisy, but at least we're still together, under one roof, even if that roof does leak. I'm grateful for what we have."

I nod in silent agreement. All day, I've been wondering why the camera chose me, and why it chose to send me to the Depression. Now I have an idea. I believe the

camera brought me here to show me how to appreciate what I have at home and how to be more compassionate. To do that, it has given me a new and wonderful friend: Kit.

❄ *To go home now,*
   turn to page 76.

❄ *To return to Kit's house,*
   turn to page 86.

I crook my arm over my face, crying as I run up the stairs. When I'm safely alone in Kit's room, I throw myself on the bed and cry hot tears of sorrow, scolding myself all the while. I mean, I knew I'd have to say good-bye to Buddy sooner or later, didn't I? I just never imagined how much it would hurt.

Will I see Buddy again? Will the camera ever let me return? At least Kit will be able to see him again. And she'll be paid, too, which will be good for her family.

"Lulu?" I hear Kit whisper. She comes over and sits on the bed next to me. "I'm so sorry about Buddy. We'll all miss him, but I know that you'll miss him most of all."

"He was never really mine," I say into the pillow.

Kit's quiet for a moment, thinking. Then she says, "Well, I'm not so sure about that. You loved him, and took care of him, and had adventures with him. He was yours for one day, and you made that day a happy one."

I roll over and look at Kit. "One day's not very much."

"No," Kit agrees. She sighs. "But it's better than nothing, and one thing I've learned from the Depression is to be glad even for a small dose of happiness. Happiness comes unexpectedly, so you'd better be on the lookout for it, otherwise you'll miss it."

"I guess I should be glad that Buddy—I mean Scooter—has such a nice owner," I say. "And that he's not far away."

"Yes," agrees Kit, "and that he is home, where he truly belongs."

I swallow hard. *Home.* Maybe it's time for me to go home, too.

"I've got to go downstairs now and help Mother," says Kit. "You rest up here awhile. Don't come down until you're ready, okay?"

"Okay." I grab Kit's hand as she stands to go. "And Kit? Thank you."

"No—thank *you*, Lulu," says Kit. "You gave all of us—not just Buddy—a happy day today."

When Kit leaves, I write her a note. It says:

Dear Kit,

I hope you won't think I am rude for going home without saying good-bye, but good-bye is a hard word to say to a good friend like you. No words can express how grateful I am for your kindness to me. I will never forget it.

With thanks and love,

Lulu

I fold the note and tuck the twenty-dollar bill inside it. Then I prop the note up on Kit's typewriter.

I take one last look around Kit's room. Then I look out the window. Outside, I see Kit, who will forever be right next to Izza in the place in my heart where I keep my best friends. And I think of Buddy—oh, Buddy—whom I will miss every day of my life.

I make myself turn away from the window. Then I put on my old coat, take a deep breath, close my eyes, and click the camera.

✺ *Turn to page 79.*

Suddenly, I know that the time has come for me to go home. Home, where I won't take things or people—especially Mom—for granted. Home, where I'll be what Kit has taught me to be: attentive, alert, and mindful. Come to think of it, don't those three things add up to being what Mom wants me to be: responsible?

But what can I do about Buddy? I can't take him home with me, and Kit already has a dog. I turn back to look at the people in the soup kitchen and see Mrs. Schultz tying a little girl's shoelaces. *That's it!* I know just what to do.

"Hey, Kit, I think Buddy and I will stay here at the soup kitchen a little longer, and then—" I take a deep breath. "And then I'll go home to my own family."

Kit's face falls. "Are you sure?"

I nod.

"Do you know how to get home?" Kit asks, sounding both sad and concerned.

Without thinking, I pat the camera. "Don't worry, I know how to get home," I tell her.

"Well, okay then," says Kit reluctantly. "I'll miss you, Lulu."

"I'll miss you, too," I say. "Please tell Uncle Hendrick thanks for sending me to your family, and I'll catch him next time I'm here." I hug Kit, and she hugs me back. "Thank you, Kit. I'll never forget today."

"Neither will I!" says Kit. She pats Buddy, hugs me again, and leaves.

I watch her until I can't see her anymore. Saying good-bye to Kit is the hardest thing I have ever done.

Then, even though it's the *second* hardest thing I've ever done, I carry Buddy over to Mrs. Schultz and say, "This dog's name is Buddy and he's—" I have to swallow hard—"he's a *really* nice dog. Do you think he could stay here with you, and be a buddy for the children who come to the soup kitchen?"

Mrs. Schultz tilts her head. "Do you mean that you want to leave him here?" she asks.

I nod because I can't speak. I kiss Buddy and put him into Mrs. Schultz's arms.

She says, "Buddy can't live here, but I know my own family would love to have him. And he can come to work with me each day to cheer up the children here at the soup kitchen." She looks straight into my eyes. All she says is, "Thank you." But the words are heartfelt.

I nod again. Then I step outside and go around the corner where no one will see me, and I click the camera.

❉ *Turn to page 81.*

When I open my eyes, I'm sitting on the floor in my room, with the camera in my hands. According to the clock, it's exactly, precisely the moment it was before I left and found myself in 1933, with Kit.

I turn on my laptop. There's the screen, just the way I left it, blank except for the title at the top:

The Most Important Idea I Learned This Summer

Now I have too many ideas for my paragraph! Should I write about generosity, friendship, courage, or determination? No—I'll write about gratitude:

This summer, I learned to be grateful for all that I have and to make the best of it. That means not taking anything for granted, and realizing that it is our responsibility to use our abilities to make what we have as good as it can be. Don't whine, but don't settle! Be creative, pay attention, and don't be afraid to try new things. You'll be surprised at what you can accomplish with determination and a little ingenuity. And you'll be surprised at how much fun it can be, too!

I'm so absorbed with my writing that I don't even

hear it when the door to my room opens.

"Hi, sweetie," says Mom. "There's someone here who wants to meet you."

She opens the door wider, and in bounds the cutest, wiggliest puppy you've ever seen. He runs up to me and jumps into my lap. When I bend my face to him, he smooches me with his wet nose. My heart is about to burst with happiness. "Oh, thank you, Mom!" I exclaim.

"Well," says Mom, "this is to thank *you*, honey. I know you weren't crazy about Camp Mosquito, but you went anyway and made the best of it. I appreciated that."

I hug the puppy. "Now I have someone to keep me company while you're at work," I tell her.

Mom smiles. "He seems to know he belongs to you. What will you name him?"

"Buddy." I think of Kit, who taught me about generosity, hard work, and gratitude, and the other Buddy, who kept me company on the adventure. The new puppy wags his tail. "Yup," I announce. "He's Buddy."

❈ *The End* ❈

To read this story another way and see how different choices lead to a different ending, turn back to page 35.

I find myself back in my room, missing Kit and Buddy so much that my heart aches. I remember how cool Kit's room was because everything had a place where it *belonged*. So I put my books on the bookshelf, my shoes in the closet, my laptop on my desk—well, once I get started putting stuff away, I sort of get really into it and the time flies by.

I'm surprised when Mom pokes her head into my room and says, "Hello, lovey! How are—" She stops and whistles. "Hey, what happened in here? Your room looks so organized!"

I shrug and grin. "A place for everything and everything in its place, right?"

"I love it!" says Mom.

I jump up and throw my arms around her. "I love you!" I say. "You're the best mother in the world."

"Only because I have the best daughter in the world," says Mom. She hugs me back. "I'm going to have a cup of tea. Would you like to join me?"

I say, "Yes, but first I have to write an essay for school."

"Ah," says Mom. "Okay. Don't hurry." She grins. "I'll wait for you, because I'd like to talk to you about

something. It seems to me that a girl who has a neat and tidy room and who is conscientious about her schoolwork might be ready to take care of a pet. Do you agree?"

I hug Mom again. I'm pretty sure there are both tears and stars in my eyes as I say, "Yes!"

❄ *The End* ❄

To read this story another way and see how different choices lead to a different ending, turn back to page 51.

K

o, Kit," I say. "Your mother has made it clear that I should go. She's been generous to me, and I don't want to repay her kindness by mooching." I pick up the sack of potatoes, and Buddy looks up at me as if he's asking, "Now what?"

Kit says sadly, "Well, at least let me walk to the hobo jungle with you."

This I agree to, since I haven't got a clue where the jungle is, or *what* it is, for that matter. I mean, the word *jungle* makes it sound as if there'll be giant ferns and monkeys.

Kit and Buddy and I set out together. I'm carrying the sack of potatoes that Mrs. Kittredge gave me. I feel phony-baloney about the potatoes. My mother doesn't cook from scratch much, or at all, really. She says her best recipe is the phone number of our favorite pizza delivery place. And the most interaction I've had with a whole potato is putting sour cream on it at a restaurant. I should give these potatoes to someone who'll know what to do with them. I ask Kit, "Have you met lots of homeless kids?"

"Oh, yes," says Kit. Her voice sounds heavy and tired. "I've met them at the hobo jungle, and at soup kitchens, and at churches where they can sleep and get clothes and food."

I have an idea. "Listen, when we get to the hobo jungle, let's give these potatoes away."

"You're sure?" asks Kit.

I nod. "That way, your mother's kindness will help more people than just me."

"That's nice of you, Lulu," says Kit. "You know, before the Depression I was just a carefree kid—and sort of selfish. I never thought about anybody but myself."

I blush. Isn't that exactly what I'm like at home—thinking only about what *I* want and how *I* feel? "So the Depression, and your dad losing his job, kind of made you grow up fast?" I ask Kit.

"Well, yes, I guess so," says Kit. "I've become more independent and—"

"Caring?" I suggest.

"I hope so," Kit says slowly. She looks at me with a sideways smile. "So I guess even the Depression isn't completely bad," she says, "if it changes people for the better."

Kit leads Buddy and me down a hill next to the train station, and instead of the ferny jungle I'm half

expecting, a secret city appears. Well, it's a city except that instead of houses there are ragged tents and rough lean-tos made out of boards. Instead of roads there are narrow dirt paths that wind between the trees and bushes. Instead of restaurants there are open fires with beat-up old cooking pots on them. It is a very sad, tumbledown secret city.

Kit and Buddy and I go up to one of the fires. A tired woman is stirring stew in a pot. Kit nudges me and nods toward the woman.

"Ma'am," I say politely, "these are for you." I hand her the sack of potatoes.

You'd think I had handed her a sack of gold. She looks at me in disbelief, and then says, "God bless you. Thank you most kindly."

"You're welcome." I smile at her, but inside I am thinking of all the food I've wasted in my life. I resolve never to be picky-persnickety about food and never, ever to waste food again.

❀ *Turn to page 93.*

K it and Buddy and I walk back to Kit's house, and when we get there, we find Mrs. Kittredge and Mrs. Howard in the kitchen folding laundry. Buddy flirts with his crush, Mrs. Howard, wagging his tail and leaning against her leg to get her attention. A small smile flits across Mrs. Howard's face so quickly I'd have missed it if I'd blinked. No question: Buddy is winning her over. *No one* can resist his bouncy cuteness!

"Hi, girls," Mrs. Kittredge says. She smiles as she hands Kit a pile of folded clothes. "Please put these away in your room, Kit." Buddy and I follow Kit as she carries the clothes up to her room in the attic. Grace is up there, waiting for us patiently.

"Your room is cool," I tell Kit.

"Does it feel cool to you?" Kit asks. She puts the laundry on the bed. "I think it's sort of hot up here."

I realize that Kit only thinks of *cool* as meaning *chilly,* not *wonderful.* Actually, the attic room is roasting hot because there's no air-conditioning, not even a fan. It's so hot that the camera strap is making my neck itchy, but I don't dare take the camera off.

"Oh, by 'cool' I mean that your room looks great," I explain.

Kit sits cross-legged on her desk chair and spins around, which makes both Buddy and Grace bark. Kit and I laugh, and then Kit stops spinning and says, "This is my favorite alcove. When I sit here, I think about being a reporter when I grow up, even though I know that not many women have jobs like that."

I smile. Just about every woman I know has a job. "You stick to your ambition," I tell Kit. "Who knows how things will change for women in the future? You should keep on writing. What do you like to write?"

Kit sits up straight and puts her hands over the keys of her typewriter. "I used to love writing a family newsletter for my dad to read when he came home from work—back when he had a job, that is. Stirling drew illustrations, and my friend Ruthie helped, too."

"Where is Ruthie now?" I ask.

"She's away visiting her grandmother," says Kit. "She'll be home in a few days."

"Well, why don't you write a newsletter for her?" I suggest. "What's new around here?"

Kit laughs aloud. "You are!" she says. "I'll write about you and Buddy."

"Okay," I say. I strike a glamorous pose. "It'll

make me feel like a movie star."

Kit starts banging away on the typewriter keys. I sit on the bed in the middle of the clean clothes and slowly unfold them one by one so that I can see them better. I put a shirt and a skirt together, and then try the shirt with some silky pajama pants, just to see how that would look. I love the feel of the fabrics as much as Kit seems to love the feel of her typewriter keys.

"Here's what I have so far," says Kit. She reads aloud:

```
She's funny, smart, friendly, and fun
to be with. Who is she? Lulu! Today our
family welcomes Lulu to our home. We
welcome Buddy, too, a lively golden re-
triever puppy that arrived at the same
time as Lulu and follows her everywhere.
Buddy has decided that he belongs to
Lulu, or maybe that Lulu belongs to him.
```

"That's really good!" I say.

"Thanks," says Kit. "Can I ask you some questions?"

"Sure," I reply. "Interview me like you're a news-

paper reporter and I'm someone famous."

"Okay," says Kit. "Let's see. Do you like sports?"

"Yes. Tennis and baseball."

"Me too!" says Kit. "Stirling and I like to play baseball, and we're big fans of Ernie Lombardi, the catcher for the Cincinnati Reds. I also like to read. Do you?"

"No, I don't like reading—I *love* reading!"

"Have you ever read *Robin Hood*?" she asks.

"Isn't he the guy who robbed the rich to give money to the poor? And his girlfriend was Maid Marian, and he and his merry band lived in the forest—"

"Up in the trees," Kit bursts in. "Someday Ruthie and Stirling and I are going to have a tree house and camp out in it."

"I've always wanted to do that, too!" No wonder Kit and I get along so well. We like a lot of the same things.

"What do you want to be when you grow up?"

"Oh, I don't know," I reply. "I don't have any special talent, really. I wish I loved writing, like you do. I wish I were good at it and it was as easy for me as it is for you. But I'm a bad speller, so I get discouraged." It's true: half the time even spell check can't tell what I'm trying to spell.

"Spelling isn't writing," says Kit. "And I work hard at writing to get better at it. Anyway, I think I know what you love."

"Buddy?" I say, picking him up and hugging him.

"Sure!" Kit laughs. "We all love Buddy. But look at yourself. I think you're right smack in the middle of what you love, right now."

I look around myself. I'm blissfully happy, surrounded by dresses and skirts and blouses that I've put together in outfits. I run my hand over the fabrics, smoothing them. "But messing around with clothes is just a hobby," I say. I think of the girls at the soup kitchen; they have no time for frivolous hobbies.

"Don't brush it off like that!" says Kit. "It's what you love to do. And remember how good you were back at the soup kitchen finding the perfect thing to fit each girl? Gosh, Lulu, you've got a talent for clothes. It seems to me that you should be proud of it!"

"I guess I never thought of it as something to be proud of."

Kit clackety-clacks away on her typewriter for a minute. "What do you think of this?"

When Lulu grows up, she will be a
fashion designer. She will design new
dresses, but she will be most famous for
the magical way she can turn tired old
clothes into new and beautiful outfits.

I blush. "Do you really think so? Do you think I can
be a dress designer when I grow up?" The idea pleases
me so much that I have goose bumps on my arms.

"Absolutely!" says Kit.

And Buddy barks, to show that he agrees, so I hug
him again.

I think, *Isn't it funny that I had to go all the way back to
1933 to find out what my future could be?*

I make up my mind right then and there that when
I return to the twenty-first century, I'll take my interest
in clothes more seriously. I know I've got a lot to learn
about fabric and design, and I'll work hard at it to get
better at it, the way Kit works at her writing. I'll unpack
my project suitcase and organize my scissors and pins
and sewing supplies, and I'll finish what I start. I'll see
if I can find a way to use the clothes I create to help
other people. After all, everyone needs clothes! Maybe

I'll donate my creations to homeless shelters, the way Kit and I donated her clothes to the girls at the soup kitchen.

My heart's beating faster, I'm so excited. I make a promise to myself that I will bring more than memories back with me from 1933. I will bring an ambition: When I grow up, I am going to be a fashion designer.

❄ *The End* ❄

To read this story another way and see how different choices lead to a different ending, turn back to page 72.

Buddy trots off to explore, so Kit and I hurry to keep up with him, stepping carefully around the ragged tents and rough lean-tos as we make our way. We've just passed by a sleeping man when the man suddenly jumps up and grabs Kit by the arm.

"What have you done with my shoes, girlie?" he asks in a raspy voice. "I know you nipped 'em and hid them somewheres. Give 'em back, or you'll be sorry."

Kit looks startled and a little frightened. "I—I didn't take your shoes," she stammers. "Honest."

"You leave her alone!" I demand. "She didn't take your shoes."

"Yes, she did," the man growls. "I saw her. She stole my shoes, and I reckon she plans to sell 'em."

"Liar!" I say. Buddy barks, and I grab the man's arm and try to wrestle it off of Kit. "You let her go!"

❈ *Turn to page 98.*

I'm nervous about going to Uncle Hendrick's house. As Kit and I walk along, the camera bounces against my chest and Buddy bounces along next to my feet.

I ask Kit, "How did Uncle Hendrick let your family know that Lucille—I mean, that I—would be coming?"

"He wrote my parents a letter. And he enclosed in it a letter to me, too." She shows me her letter.

"May I read it?" I'm hoping I'll be able to tell from the letter whether Uncle Hendrick has ever met Lucille.

Kit hesitates. "It's kind of a gruff letter."

I can tell that Kit is trying to protect me. "Don't worry. No matter what he says about me, it won't hurt my feelings."

Kit sighs and hands me the typed letter. I unfold it and read:

201 Chestnut Court
Cincinnati, Ohio
August 25, 1933

Kit,

It is most annoying and inconvenient,
but my distant grand-niece, Lucille, is
coming to Cincinnati. I have no interest
in hosting her, and since she's your age
it would be better for her to stay with
your family. You and that pipsqueak boy
Stirling can amuse her. It will give you
a chance to do something useful for a
change. I have far too many things to do,
and all of them are far more important
than playing mother hen to some silly
young girl, you can be sure!

I'll pay for Lucille's room and board,
which I am sure your parents will welcome
since they're desperate for money and since
they're foolishly and stubbornly insisting
on pursuing your mother's terrible idea
of running a boardinghouse. You mark my
words: the boardinghouse will never earn
enough money to pay the mortgage or send
your brother Charlie to college.

Sincerely,
Uncle Hendrick

"Whew," I whistle. "Gruff is right."

"Well, you know how Uncle Hendrick is," says Kit.

Actually, no, I don't. But I can't tell Kit that. For all
I know, Lucille has met Uncle Hendrick hundreds of
times. "What does Uncle Hendrick mean about paying
the mortgage?" I ask. "What is a mortgage, anyway?"

"A mortgage is like rent, only you pay it to the bank
every month," Kit explains. "Our mortgage is twenty
dollars a month, and if we don't pay it, we'll get kicked
out of our house."

"That's awful!" I exclaim. Kit's family is on the
verge of being homeless! "And what does Uncle Hendrick mean about Charlie and college?"

"Charlie was supposed to go to college to study
English literature. But he couldn't, because there's no
money to pay for his tuition."

"That's so unfair!"

"There's nothing fair about the Depression," says
Kit. "But President Roosevelt is trying to make things
better. He started lots of programs to give people jobs.
Charlie works for one of them, the Civilian Conservation Corps. Charlie joined up and went to Montana to
work at Glacier National Park planting trees and build-

ing roads. The money he sends home helps a lot. His leave will be over soon, and I'll miss him terribly when he goes back out west."

All of a sudden, boy, do I miss my mom. I've never really thought about money before, and I've always stubbornly resented how much my mother works. But now, listening to Kit, I suddenly understand how hard my mom works to give me everything I could need or want, now or in the future, like going to college. I can't imagine how scary it must be to live in constant fear of being homeless, like the Kittredges.

I have a brainstorm. What if I click the camera and go back to my time and gather up all the cash I can find and bring it back for Kit's family? They need the money. I don't. No one ever cares how I spend my money. I've got my $35 of birthday gift money from my grand-mother in my piggy bank and plenty of spare change.

❈ To go home and get money,
turn to page 100.

❈ To stay here with Kit,
turn to page 104.

Desperately, Kit wrenches her arm away from the mean man. *"Run!"* she orders.

Buddy and I don't need to be told twice. We run as fast as we can away from the man, darting around the people in our way, hopping over boxes and rotting logs, ducking under makeshift clotheslines. Up toward the train tracks we struggle. But the man is so close on our heels, it is as if I can feel him breathing down my neck.

"In here!" yells Kit. She climbs into a boxcar and leans out, shouting, "Give me Buddy!"

I scoop up Buddy, more or less toss him to Kit, and then fling myself headfirst into the boxcar. Before I can even turn around, the car starts to move! The man chases the train for a while, but as we pick up speed he falls farther and farther behind until he gives up. We see him shaking his fist. He's yelling, but we can't hear him over the rattle and bang of the car.

"Full speed ahead!" I shout, thrilled by our victorious getaway. Then I turn to Kit. "Where are we going?"

"Don't worry," pants Kit. "The train will stop. It's just changing tracks."

But Kit is wrong. The train thunders along, faster and faster. Kit and I clutch each other as we look out

the door at the trees and hillsides flying by.

"Oh no," I hear Kit moan. I can see why. The train is whizzing across a bridge that spans a river far below.

I'm so scared that I think of clicking the camera to go home. But I can't desert Kit and Buddy.

We sink back into the gloomy darkness of the car. There is nothing to do and nothing to say. We are trapped in the boxcar until the train stops, whenever and wherever that may be.

❇ *Turn to page 101.*

K it and Buddy pop into the post office to mail a letter. The second they are gone, I click the camera and go home to the twenty-first century to look for money.

Gosh, my room is chaotic! Stuff's everywhere. I rummage around, searching for my purse and my piggy bank. The next time I return to the twenty-first century, I vow to clean and organize my room really well. But right now, I need to get back to Kit.

Finally, I find my purse and dig out some money. But when I look at it, I realize my twenty-first-century money will not help the Kittredges. It has the date on it, and that date would freak everyone out in the 1930s. They'd think it was counterfeit. I'll have to find another way to help them.

I click the camera to hurry back to Kit and Buddy. They're just coming out of the post office.

❈ *Turn to page 104.*

Buddy wiggles his way out of my arms and skitters farther into the boxcar.

"Why, hello there, pup," I hear a voice say.

I squint into the blackness. In a far corner, I see an old man petting Buddy. He smiles at Kit and me. "Hello to you, too," he says. "I didn't know I'd be having company on the train. I'm Mr. Birdseye. How do?" He holds out his hand, so I shake it as we introduce ourselves.

"I'm Lulu," I say. "And this is Kit."

"Nice to meet you," says Mr. Birdseye. "Welcome aboard."

"Thanks," I say.

"Mr. Birdseye," says Kit, "can you tell us where this train is going?"

"South," says Mr. Birdseye. "We just crossed the river into Kentucky."

"Kentucky?" I squeak.

"Does this train stop in Mountain Hollow?" Kit asks nervously.

"First Poncton," says Mr. Birdseye. "Then Mountain Hollow."

Kit turns to me. "My Aunt Millie lives in Mountain Hollow, Kentucky," she says, trying to reassure me. "If

we can get there, she'll help us get back to Cincinnati."

As the train lurches along, Mr. Birdseye uses a piece of chalk to show Kit and me some hobo symbols. "You need to know these if you're going to get home safely," he says.

He draws the symbols on the floor of the boxcar.

"This one means 'good jungle,' and this one means 'jail or prison.'"

Just then, with a sickening screech of its brakes, the train slows and then skids to a halt.

Mr. Birdseye holds his finger to his lips. "Shh," he whispers. "It's probably a couple of bulls."

"The train stopped for cattle?" I ask.

"No, railroad bulls," says Mr. Birdseye softly. "They're men the railroad hires to throw tramps like us off the trains."

Kit, Buddy, Mr. Birdseye, and I cower in a huddle in the darkest corner of the boxcar as we hear men's voices coming closer and closer. The door to our boxcar is slid open all the way, and a deep voice says, "We know you bums are in there. Come on out before we climb in and haul you out."

Kit and I hold our breath and look at Mr. Birdseye.

With a sigh, he slowly stands up. Blinking as we walk from the shadows into the glaring sunlight, Mr. Birdseye, Kit, and I stumble to the door.

Two big men shake their heads when they see Kit and me. "Kids," one man mutters, disgusted. "Just kids."

Mr. Birdseye jumps down, and then he helps Kit and me to the ground. Buddy jumps into my arms. The railroad bulls clamp heavy hands on our shoulders and make us walk in front of them. "Come on," they say, shoving us. "Get moving."

❀ *To cooperate with the bulls,*
   turn to page 106.

❀ *To run away,*
   turn to page 130.

❀ *To head for Mountain Hollow,*
   go online to **beforever.com/endings**

K it hands me a nickel for the trolley. It looks different from any nickel I've ever seen. It has a buffalo on one side and a Native American on the other. Also, the date on the nickel is 1928. So of course my modern money would be useless here.

The trolley stop is on a busy corner with cars rushing by, trucks spewing smoke, horns honking, and people jostling one another. *Screeech!* The trolley arrives and stops in front of us with a deafening squeal of brakes. People spill out onto the sidewalk.

"Come on," says Kit. "Let's get on the trolley."

I hesitate. An obnoxious bell on the trolley starts to clang so loudly that I can't hear myself think. It's freaking out Buddy, too, so I pick him up in my arms.

"What's the matter?" asks Kit, shouting over the bell. "Haven't you ever ridden a trolley before?"

I shake my head no. "My mom drives me in her car," I say, and then regret it. Whenever I say something that makes me sound pampered and privileged, it puts a distance between Kit and me.

"Hurry up!" says Kit. "We'll miss the trolley!" She climbs aboard, and I'm right behind her. We pay our fares. But then, disaster! The trolley bell clangs

again, and Buddy jumps out of my arms and disappears down the street!

"Buddy!" Kit and I yell at the top of our lungs.

❇ *To jump off and chase after Buddy,*
   turn to page 112.

❇ *To sit tight and stay on the trolley with Kit,*
   turn to page 118.

We stumble down the embankment, across a field, and onto a narrow paved road. It's swelteringly hot, poor Buddy is exhausted, and I'm really tired and thirsty, but the bulls won't let us stop and rest.

Eventually, we come to a small town. A painted sign says "Welcome to Lewis Falls! We're glad you're here!" which makes me want to snort, "Well, *I'm* not!" Kit pokes me. She points to a hobo symbol scratched onto the sign. We both recognize it as the symbol that means *jail*.

Sure enough, the bulls soon usher us into a red brick building, and my heart sinks when I see the sign by the door: *Lewis Falls Jail*. When I used to dream of adventure, I never dreamed of being put in jail.

At least it's cooler inside the jail, and I must say that it's as clean as a whistle. The bulls put Mr. Birdseye in a jail cell with some other men. They're about to put Kit and me in a cell when a stout lady bustles toward us.

"Great balls of fire, Lucius!" the stout lady scolds the tallest bull. "You can't put those two young 'uns in a cell. Why, they're just babies."

Lucius looks stubborn. "Babies who hopped a freight," he grunts. "Broke the law."

"Never you mind!" says the lady. Her round, red
face is determined. "You give those girls over to me or
you'll regret it for a month of Sundays."

Lucius shrugs, gives Kit and me a little nudge
toward the lady, and stalks off in a huff.

"There now, there now," says the stout lady to Kit
and me. "Sit you down, girls."

Kit and I sit on a bench, and the lady gives us cups
of water from the water cooler. She even fills a cup for
Buddy. When we've finished, she says, "I can tell by the
look of you that there's someone at home who's mighty
worried about the pair of you, and your sweet pup."
She hands Kit a nickel and gestures toward a pay telephone on the wall, saying, "Borrow this nickel, and call
someone to come fetch you."

"Thank you," says Kit. "Thank you very much."

The lady beams at us. "Nice polite girls," she says.
"I knew it."

"Are you going to call your parents?" I ask Kit as
the lady leaves.

Kit sighs. "We don't have a car. And we don't have
a phone at our house because we couldn't afford it anymore," she says. "There's only one person I could call

who has a car *and* a phone: Uncle Hendrick. It's long
distance, so I'll have to call him collect. He'll fuss and
fume, but he's my only choice."

I haven't met Uncle Hendrick. He sounds grumpy,
but I won't care how much he fusses and fumes as long
as he comes to the rescue—and soon. I'm afraid if we
stick around much longer, Lucius will put us in a cell
no matter what the stout lady says!

Kit looks unhappy about it, but she calls Uncle
Hendrick. After she hangs up, she says, "He's mad. But
he's coming. Charlie is going to drive him here." Then
she returns the nickel to the lady.

While we wait outside in the shade of the jail, I ask
Kit, "Who is Uncle Hendrick?"

Kit sighs. "He's my mother's uncle. He lives in a big,
fancy house all by himself. He never misses a chance to
criticize our family."

"Uncle Hendrick sounds annoying," I say. "He
sounds kind of like my Aunt Shelly, who once told
me I needed a manicure. But I'll be happy to meet
Charlie."

"Oh, you'll like Charlie!" says Kit. "He's great. He's
home on leave from the Civilian Conservation Corps.

He's helping build roads and bridges in Glacier Park,
Montana."

"Listen, Kit," I say. "When Uncle Hendrick and
Charlie get here, I think Buddy and I should say good-
bye and go our own way. We—"

"No!" Kit says fiercely. "Please come back to
Cincinnati with me. I can't just leave you and Buddy
alone out here."

"Okay," I say, secretly relieved. I don't want to
say good-bye to Kit one second sooner than I need to!
Also, I don't have a brother myself, so I'm curious about
Charlie. I ask Kit, "Does Charlie like working in
Montana?"

"Yes, I think so," says Kit. "And I know he's proud
that he's helping our family with the money he sends
home every month. Before the Depression, Charlie's
dream was to go to college and study English literature.
But then Dad lost his job, so of course there's no money
for college."

"How much is tuition?"

"Forty-five dollars a year," Kit says. "Nearly two
hundred dollars for all four years." She shakes her head
at the staggering impossibility of the sum.

I happen to know that the college my lunkhead cousin Jayden goes to costs forty-five *thousand* dollars a year because my Aunt Shelly—the one who said I needed a manicure—is always whining-but-really-bragging about it. But I understand that to Kit's family, forty-five dollars might as well be a million.

I'm impressed when Kit sits up straighter and looks me in the eye. "Someday, somehow, I'm going to figure out a way to pay for Charlie to go to college."

"If anybody can do it, you can," I tell her, and I mean it with all my heart. "And what about you? Wouldn't you like to go to college, too?"

Kit nods. She speaks quietly, as if she's telling a secret wish. "I'd like to go to college and study journalism. I want to be a reporter when I grow up." She sighs. "But I might as well ask for the moon."

Now *I* have a secret wish—that I could make it possible for Kit to go to college. I mean, it just burns me up that my cousin Jayden, who seems to be majoring in skateboarding, can go to college and Kit and Charlie can't.

After a long time, a big, fancy car pulls up. A good-looking guy who is obviously Charlie is driving, and a

cranky-looking codger who has to be Uncle Hendrick is sitting like a king in the back.

Charlie jumps out and picks up Kit in a swinging hug. Kit introduces me to Charlie, and he grins at me. "Lulu," he says, "for a pint-sized girl you seem to stir up a lot of trouble."

I blush. Why do I always look the most ridiculous when I least want to?

"Come along!" barks Uncle Hendrick, who does not even bother to get out of the car. "I don't have all day."

Kit runs inside and is back in a flash. We all clamber into the car.

"Hold that mutt in your lap!" Uncle Hendrick orders when he gets a load of Buddy. "I don't want him shedding all over the upholstery!"

I pick up Buddy, and we're off.

❧ *Turn to page 113.*

Without thinking, I jump off the trolley after Buddy. Too late, I realize that Kit isn't with me. "Kit!" I yell frantically. She sees me, but the trolley's going too fast for her to jump off. *"Kit!"* I shriek again.

Kit shouts at me, but I can't hear her over the racket of the trolley's clanging bell and screeching metal wheels. The trolley disappears, and Kit disappears with it.

I'm left all alone on a street corner. I have no idea where I am, and I have no idea how to get back to Kit's house, or even what her address is. I'm lost in a place I don't know, in a time I don't know, and I'm pretending to be a girl I don't know. I am completely, utterly, totally lost.

❈ *Turn to page 120.*

Before we can heave a sigh of relief, Uncle Hendrick begins to scold us. Pretty soon, it begins to feel as if the jail cell would have been a more peaceful place to be.

"I don't like to drive," says Uncle Hendrick, "so I had to corral Charlie into driving my car to the back of beyond to fetch you two hooligans." He glares at me. "Who are you, by the way?"

"She's my friend Lulu," says Kit bravely.

"What kind of a name is that?" scowls Kit's uncle. "Sounds like a birdcall. I'm not going to say that I am pleased to meet you, Lulu, because I am *not*. I suppose this whole escapade was your idea. Perhaps you'll be so kind as to pay me back for the collect call! I know Kit and her family don't have a penny, much less thirty cents."

I begin to say, "I—"

But Uncle Hendrick talks right over me. "I told Kit's father not to buy that ridiculous house, but did he listen to me? No. And *now* see what's happened. He's lost his job. Kit's mother, my own niece, is reduced to a chambermaid running that boardinghouse, and Charlie here has become a common laborer, a lumberjack or some such, out in the wilds of Montana. Here he is home for leave

and can't get a job for love or money. Probably never will."

Charlie's neck reddens with anger, but he says nothing.

"Charlie is going to go to college," says Kit boldly, "when the Depression is over."

"Hunh!" scoffs Uncle Hendrick. "At the rate your family is going, Charlie will never get to college."

Kit slides me a look as if to say, *See what I mean?*

I've had it with Uncle Hendrick's bullying. I try not to be rude, but as firmly as I can I say, "I don't think that's true. The Kittredges are resourceful. They'll figure out a way."

Uncle Hendrick looks at me, flabbergasted. He's so surprised, it's as if I'm Buddy talking. I can tell he is not accustomed to being contradicted. But I face him right back. Kit is my friend, and I won't let anybody speak unfairly about her or her family.

Uncle Hendrick explodes in a rant: "Even the job Charlie has now is not a real job. It's just a make-work boondoggle cooked up by that lunatic in the White House, Roosevelt. The sooner we get rid of him and his busybody wife, Eleanor, the better. They're ruining the country."

My ears perk up. I know something about Franklin and Eleanor Roosevelt. Suddenly, I have a brainstorm.

"Uncle Hendrick," I say, "I want to make you a bet."

"Impudent whippersnapper!" sniffs Uncle Hendrick. "What sort of bet?"

"If Roosevelt is re-elected, you'll pay for Charlie to go to college. And if Roosevelt is elected two more times after that, you'll pay for Kit to go to college."

Uncle Hendrick chortles. "I'm glad to take that bet!" he says. "First of all, that man in the White House is so terrible he'll be lucky if he's not impeached. He'll never be re-elected. And secondly, no president has ever been elected to a third term, much less a fourth."

I shrug. "We'll see," I say. "If I'm wrong, Kit and Charlie will do chores for you—for free—for a *year*." I stick out my hand. "Shake on the deal?"

We shake, and Uncle Hendrick chuckles merrily to himself for the rest of the ride home, practically rubbing his hands together with glee because he is so positive that he's going to win our bet. When we reach his house, he proclaims, "I'm not going to pamper you by delivering you to your doorstep. This is far enough! As previously stated, I do *not* like to drive."

Kit's face lights up. As if she is emboldened by my example, she says, "Charlie is going to be home on leave for another two weeks. Since he doesn't have a job, let's make the best of it. While he's here, he can drive you wherever you want to go."

"Fine!" Uncle Hendrick snaps.

"But you'll have to pay him," Kit adds.

"All right, all right!" says Uncle Hendrick, sounding very testy. "He can begin by earning back the thirty cents you owe me." Uncle Hendrick acts impatient, but I think he's actually happy about Kit's proposal, or he wouldn't have agreed so quickly.

I know that Charlie is happy, because as we walk home from Uncle Hendrick's house, he says, "Kit, I owe you one! Talk about making the best of your situation. That was a stroke of genius." He turns to me. "And thank you for trying, Lulu. I appreciate how you stood up to Uncle Hendrick for Kit and me, even though there's no way in the world we'll win that bet."

"Oooh, I wouldn't be so sure," I say. "In fact, if I were you, I'd dust off my books and get cracking! And college is in *your* future too, Kit."

Kit and Charlie just laugh. But I notice that Kit has

a skip in her step, and Charlie's whistling a tune that sounds like a college fight song.

When we get back to the Kittredges' house, Kit and Charlie rush to the kitchen to tell their parents that Uncle Hendrick is going to hire Charlie as his driver. Buddy goes with them. I feel like it's their private family time, so I hang back and sit on the back porch, looking at the vegetable garden.

It's nice to feel the breeze on my face. Behind me, I can hear the Kittredges all happy and laughing together. Suddenly, I miss my mom.

Buddy will be fine with Kit and her family, I realize. It's time for me to go home.

I find a scrap of paper and a pencil on a table by the door and dash off a quick note saying good-bye and thank you to Kit and her family. Then I pick up the camera.

❊ *Turn to page 123.*

Kit and I are both just frozen. We look out the back of the fast-moving trolley, hoping against hope to see Buddy.

"Oh, Kit," I wail. "What'll we do, what'll we *do*? We've *got* to find Buddy!"

Kit looks as upset as I feel, but she takes a brave, shuddery breath and says, "We'll get off at the very next stop. We'll find Buddy. Don't you worry, Lulu."

I really admire how Kit does not panic. Maybe when terrible things happen to you, like your dad losing his job, you learn how to keep your cool.

The trolley stops after only a few blocks, and Kit and I hop off. We run as fast as we can back to the spot where Buddy jumped out of my arms.

There is no trace of Buddy. He has disappeared. "Where could he have gone?" I moan. "Oh, we're *never* going to find him."

"Yes, we will," Kit says firmly. "We'll walk all over Cincinnati if we have to." She grabs my hand. "Let's go."

Kit and I trudge up and down hill after hill after hill, calling Buddy and asking everyone we meet if they've seen a golden retriever puppy. We look in parks, front yards, parking lots, alleys, backyards,

lobbies of apartment buildings, shops, restaurants, garages, and office buildings. Finally, our feet give out. We collapse on a park bench in a plaza that surrounds a fountain.

Kit swipes her sweaty forehead with the back of her hand. "We're not giving up," she says. "But let's go to Uncle Hendrick's and get that over with. Then we can search for Buddy some more."

"Okay," I say. I'm so hot and tired and discouraged that I want to cry. Oh, my Buddy—how could I have lost you? Now I understand completely what Mom meant when she said that having a pet is a big deal. Losing Buddy is the biggest deal and the worst thing I've ever faced.

❋ *Turn to page 125.*

Heart pounding, I run in the direction that I saw Buddy go. I've got to find him. If anything happens to Buddy, I'll never forgive myself. This must be what Mom meant about a pet being a big responsibility. I dash across the street and run around the corner, where I practically collide with a horse-drawn wagon.

A horse-drawn wagon? Have I traveled even farther back in time? Am I now in pioneer days? What's next, a buffalo?

But the houses and cars on the street haven't changed, and as I come around the wagon, there's Buddy, buddying up to a large gray horse. A rather raggedy-looking man is squatting next to Buddy, petting him with a friendly smile.

I run to Buddy and scoop him up. "Buddy! Oh, I'm so glad to see you!"

Buddy licks my face and squirms with puppyish joy in my arms.

"Hello, young miss," says the raggedy man. He tips his old, chewed-up straw hat as he stands. "Looks like your dog is glad to see *you*, too."

"I thought he was lost!" I hug Buddy again. "Of

course, now we're *both* lost."

"Well," says the man, "being lost just means that you're not where you want to be. Where do you *want* to be?"

"I'm staying with the Kittredges," I tell him. "Do you know where they live?"

"No," says the man. "Sorry. Cincinnati is a big city. Thousands of people live here. Do you have an address?"

"No," I sigh.

Wait! I put my hand in my pocket and oh, *hurray!* I pull out Uncle Hendrick's letter, and, sure enough, it has his address on it. I hold it out to the man. "Please, can you tell me how to get to Chestnut Court?"

"I can do better than that. I can give you a ride there," he says. "Hop up onto the wagon."

I lift Buddy onto the wagon seat. The man climbs up, and then reaches a hand to me, and I scramble up onto the seat. Buddy perches between us, happy as can be.

The horse *clip-clops* along at a pretty brisk pace under the leafy trees and then into patches of bright sunshine. It's really nice to ride uncovered, feeling the

breeze on my face. It's like riding in a convertible, or on a float in a parade.

"What do you collect in your wagon?" I ask the man.

"Rags," he answers. "I buy the rags and then sell them to factories that make paper from them."

I grin. "We call that recycling where I come from." It even sort of reminds me of how I like to turn old clothes into new ones.

Pretty soon we turn the corner onto a street of big, stately homes. The ragman stops in front of Number 201 Chestnut Court. "Very fancy!" he says. "Are you sure this is where you want to go?"

Honestly? No, I want to say. I'm afraid to meet Uncle Hendrick. But Kit might be at his house, so I've got to face my fear and go there.

❧ *Turn to page 128.*

I am back in my room. Everything is exactly as it was before I left on my adventure—but *I'm* different. I've known how sweet it is to have a pet to love, and my heart has a painful empty space in it now. Oh, how I miss Kit and lovable Buddy!

I wander out into the living room. My babysitter, Sophie, is there on the couch. I wave to her, and she pulls her earphones off.

"Hi," she says, a little uncertainly.

"Um, hi, Sophie," I reply. Then I think about how some of the people Kit and I met were friendly to us. Despite our scruffy appearance, they helped us instead of judging us too swiftly. Maybe I have judged Sophie too swiftly. Maybe she hasn't been ignoring me; maybe *I* have been ignoring *her*.

"Hey, by any chance do you have a pet at home?" I ask her.

Sophie breaks into a smile a mile wide. "Yes," she says. "I have a dog from a rescue shelter. He's a real sweetheart. He's little and shy, so we named him Brave-heart to build up his confidence."

I smile back, and then ask, "Do you think—I mean, if my mom says it's okay—would you bring Braveheart

when you come to sit for me sometimes?"

"Oh, I'd love to!" says Sophie. "And Braveheart will love it, too."

"Great!" I say, suddenly feeling excited at the prospect of getting to know my babysitter. The funny thing about it, of course, is that she was here all the time, but I just never thought about trying to get to know her.

It was Kit who showed me how smart it is to make the best of a situation. I might not have my own dog, but I'll be able to play with my sitter's dog, which will be fun. And I have a feeling that spending time with Sophie will be fun, too, if I give it a chance.

❈ *The End* ❈

To read this story another way and see how different choices lead to a different ending, turn back to page 103.

With hearts as heavy as our feet, Kit and I trudge to Uncle Hendrick's house.

When we finally get there, my courage fails me. Uncle Hendrick is sure to know that I am not his grand-niece Lucille. As we turn up his front walk, my steps are dragging. Even his door knocker scares me—it's in the shape of a dragon's head with its mouth open and a tongue of fire sticking out. Welcoming it's not. I stammer, "Kit, let's—let's just go. Please!"

Kit squeezes my hand. "It won't be so bad, I promise." She lifts the unfriendly dragon's nose and knocks on the door. She knocks and knocks, but there's no answer. "I guess Uncle Hendrick isn't home," she says at last.

Thank goodness. "Oh, well," I say casually. "It doesn't matter. We can come back later for, um, the suitcase."

Kit shakes her head. "That'd be wasting the trolley fare. Besides, we still need to find Buddy. And Mom needs me to do my chores at home. But don't worry, I know where Uncle Hendrick hides an extra key. We can let ourselves into his house and get your suitcase. I'll just leave him a note to let him know."

"Good plan," I say. Any plan that does not involve meeting Uncle Hendrick sounds like a winner to me.

Kit stands on tiptoe, pulls out a key from behind one of the porch lamps, and opens the door. We step inside. Ahead of us, I see a room full of books, and I mean *full*. Bookshelves crowded with books of all shapes and sizes line every wall from floor to ceiling, just like a library. "Wow," I gasp.

"I know," Kit says. "I think Uncle Hendrick has every book in the world! But come on, we'd better head home. We can ask Charlie to help us search for Buddy some more."

Kit walks over to a suitcase that's in the front hall. I'm sort of surprised to see it, but I guess it makes sense that the suitcase exists. After all, there is an actual Cousin Lucille somewhere who is supposed to come visit Uncle Hendrick. The letter that Uncle Hendrick wrote about her is real, so it's logical that her suitcase is real, too, and that it was sent to his house. But what happens when the true Lucille shows up?

"We'll take turns carrying the suitcase," Kit says, picking it up.

I shrug and nod, feeling a little odd about taking

someone else's suitcase, but not sure how to explain this to Kit. I also notice that the suitcase doesn't have any wheels. Will they let us take it on the trolley? If not, it will be a long schlep home, that's for sure.

"*Stop, thieves!*" an angry voice shouts.

❈ *Turn to page 132.*

I smile a weak smile and nod to the ragman. "Thank you!" I say as Buddy and I jump off the wagon.

"*Lulu!* Oh, Lulu!" someone calls. It's Kit. She runs up and gives me a hug. She's as glad to see Buddy and me as we are to see her. "I thought you were lost forever!"

"Me too," I say. "If not for the ragman, I might have been!"

The ragman waves as his horse trots away.

Kit gives Buddy a loving pat on the head. Then she smiles at me and says, "I can tell that you're not any happier about seeing Uncle Hendrick than I am, but we might as well get it over with. Come on, let's knock on the door."

We go up the steps to the door, which looks as big and dark and unfriendly as a door in a Frankenstein movie. I'm not kidding: the knocker is shaped like a fire-breathing dragon. Brave Kit grabs the dragon's snout and gives the door a good knock.

Creak. The heavy door opens, and we step inside into a cold, murky darkness. A tall, gray-haired man looms up out of the shadows and peers at us.

"Kit," he says. His face is as sour as a pickle. "What do you want?" Without waiting for an answer, he frowns at me and asks, "And who on earth are you?"

"Hi, Uncle Hendrick. She's Cousin Lucille, of course," says Kit.

"No," says Uncle Hendrick. "She is *not* Lucille."

❋ *Turn to page 135.*

Look!" shouts Mr. Birdseye to the railroad bulls. When they turn to see what he is pointing to, Mr. Birdseye turns to Kit and me and whispers, "*Go!*"

We make a dash for freedom, with Buddy hot on our heels. We run as far and as fast as we can, across a stubbly field and through a little orchard. We don't know where we're going, only that we're going *away* from the boxcar and the railroad bulls.

After a while, I look back. "I don't think they're chasing us," I say to Kit, panting.

"I guess not," says Kit, slowing down. "They're probably glad to have us off their hands."

We walk along a dusty road into a little town. A sign says, "Welcome to Lewis Falls! We're glad you're here."

It might as well say, Welcome to Timbuktu! "Kit," I ask, "how are we going to get home?"

Kit squares her shoulders. "Well," she says stoutly, "we'll just have to come up with some way to earn the train fare back to Cincinnati." I know that she's as tired and as worried as I am, but she doesn't show it. I guess if you live during the Depression, you've got to face difficulties straight on. Actually, I guess that's true no matter *when* you live. Maybe I should try it.

We're walking past a general store. Its doors are open, and they must have a lunch counter inside, because the delicious smells of coffee and apple pie waft out. We're so hungry that we can't resist going in. Of course, we have no money to pay for any food, which makes the hunger pangs hurt even more.

"May I help you?" asks a woman who's restocking the shelves with cans.

"Actually, ma'am, we're hoping that *we* can help *you*," says Kit. She sounds chipper and brisk, even though I know she's as hungry and worn-out as I am. "We need to earn train fare. Are there any chores we could do?"

The woman hesitates. I can tell that she is a nice person who would like to help us if she could. But she says, "Oh, honey, the only chore needin' doin' is to scrub out the fryin' pans. But they're so greasy and foul, I wouldn't ask my worst enemy to scrub 'em."

"Okay, thanks anyway!" I say breezily. I pick up Buddy and turn to go, but Kit stops me.

"This may be our only chance," she says fiercely. "We'd better grab it."

❧ *Turn to page 139.*

tartled, I jump about a foot. Kit and I spin around and face a squinting, suspicious woman standing on the front porch.

"What are you two hooligans up to?" she asks, hands on hips. "Get away from there or I'll call the police!"

"But I'm Kit Kittredge," Kit says bravely. "This is my Uncle Hendrick's house."

"Ha!" scoffs the woman. "I've been Hendrick Frosbythe's neighbor for thirty years and I've never seen *you* before. Hendrick would never have such a ragamuffin for a niece."

I put my hand in my pocket. "I have a letter that will explain everything," I tell the woman. But my pocket is empty.

"Oh, Kit," I gasp. "I've lost Uncle Hendrick's letter."

Kit is undaunted. "Anyway, we're not thieves, ma'am!"

"Is this your house?" asks the woman. "Is that your suitcase?"

Kit looks at me. I know she expects me to pipe up and say that the suitcase belongs to me. But I can't lie, so I don't say anything.

"This isn't my house," Kit says finally, "and that isn't my suitcase. It belongs to—"

But the woman cuts her off. "Breaking into an empty house and taking things that don't belong to you makes you thieves in my book." She looks us up and down, scowling at my well-worn clothes. "You're up to no good, I can tell. Hoboes, the two of you, is my guess. I never trust hoboes. Tramps, bums, and thieves, all of them. I've a good mind to haul you both off to the police station. But if you put that suitcase down and go back to the jungle where you belong, I'll let you go."

I whisper to Kit, "What's a hobo? What's the jungle?"

"Hoboes travel from town to town looking for work," says Kit. "Their camps near the railroad tracks are called jungles."

"Lady," I say, "you have made a mistake. My friend and I are not homeless hoboes, and even if we were, you would have no right to be mean to us."

The woman sort of gasps. I can tell that she thinks I am very rude. Probably children in the 1930s don't speak to grown-ups so boldly. But I am from the twenty-first century, and I know all about bullies. The

only way to stop them is to stand up to them.

Only it doesn't work this time. "That's enough out of you," states the woman. "Let's go. I'm marching you two sticky-fingered no-goods back to the jungle, back where you belong."

❈ *To run away,*
turn to page 145.

❈ *To go to the hobo jungle,*
turn to page 160.

Kit looks shocked, and a little annoyed at Uncle Hendrick for being rude to me.

But I'm thinking, *Uh-oh. This is what I was dreading.* Uncle Hendrick knows the real Lucille, and so he knows that I am a fake, phony imposter. I feel like the word FRAUD is printed across my forehead.

What can I say that won't be a lie? I'm so queasy-uneasy that my palms start to sweat.

Kit, however, meets Uncle Hendrick's icy gaze and replies evenly, "Sometimes when you haven't seen people in a long time, you hardly recognize them. When was the last time you saw Cousin Lucille?"

"Harumph," says Uncle Hendrick. Kit's right, but it would pain him to admit it. He scowls at me and says, "I haven't seen you since you were a bothersome little tot. You've changed, and thank goodness. I see you have a ridiculous dog with you. Your mother didn't say you'd be bringing a dog. How is your mother?"

"Um, she's fine," I say. "Working hard, as usual."

"Harumph," says Uncle Hendrick again. "I should have known that your mother hasn't changed," he gripes. "These modern women! All this rushing around! Your mother should have taken my advice and

stayed at home instead of going to college and filling her head with nonsense. Now she's wasting her energy at work. But she is as headstrong about her job as Kit's mother is about her foolish boardinghouse scheme." He glowers at Kit and says with disdain, "It will fail, like everything your family does. You mark my words."

Kit gets a stubborn look on her face. I can tell that she is really mad that Uncle Hendrick is criticizing her family. We learned about standing up to bullies in school, and Uncle Hendrick is a bully if I ever saw one. I whisper to Kit, "Stand up to him!"

Kit speaks up. "Excuse me, Uncle Hendrick," she says. "But we will *not* fail. Our boardinghouse is full. And besides—" she grins and glances at me—"it's *fun* having boarders."

"That's telling him!" I whisper.

But I can see that Uncle Hendrick is about to explode, so I try to take the heat off Kit. "I *do* wish *my* mother weren't always so busy," I say quickly—and honestly.

Uncle Hendrick turns to me. "You seem sensible," he says. "I've decided that you should move in here. I could use someone to fetch and carry for me. You look

strong and not entirely dim-witted and useless." He looks down his nose at Kit. "Don't worry, I'll still pay your parents the money I promised for Lucille's board."

Kit looks cross but says nothing.

I don't want to stay with Uncle Hendrick. He is thoroughly disagreeable, even if his house is fancy and—I look behind him—full of intriguing-looking books. On the other hand, if I stay with him, Kit's family would have the money without the expense of feeding me. Maybe staying here would be the best way for me to help the Kittredges.

While I'm trying to decide if I should stay or not, and if not, how to say "no thank you" politely, Buddy begins to growl. He sounds pretty scary for such a little pup.

"Hey, Buddy," I say, "what's the matter?"

Then I see the fattest, most unpleasant-looking Scottie dog ever lurking behind Uncle Hendrick and glowering at Buddy with glittering black eyes. *Grrr*, the Scottie growls. Then he explodes into a shrill chorus of *yip, yip, yip!*

Quickly, before the dogs lunge at each other, Kit lifts Buddy to safety in her arms. "Be quiet, Inky!" she

scolds the nasty-looking Scottie.

Ignoring the dogs completely, Uncle Hendrick opens his wallet. "It's settled, then," he says to Kit. "Lucille will stay here. Here's the money I promised. Take it to your mother."

Kit's eyes widen as he hands her a twenty-dollar bill. I know what a huge help that money will be to her family. Twenty dollars is a whole month's mortgage.

My head tells me that staying here with Uncle Hendrick is the right thing to do—but my heart says, *Stay with Kit.*

❉ *To stay with the cash-strapped Kittredges, turn to page 147.*

❉ *To stay with Uncle Hendrick, turn to page 156.*

We'd be grateful for the job, ma'am," says Kit. "And I promise that we'll do it well."

"All righty, then," says the woman, shaking her head. She leads us to a big sink behind the lunch counter. It's near the back door and it faces the wall so that we have our backs to the lunch counter, but we're still in the same room with the lady. The sink is piled high with greasy pots and pans. "Don't say I didn't warn you," she says.

Gross. I pick up a scrub cloth with the tips of my fingers as if it's a live snake.

Buddy lies down next to the sink while Kit bustles about, industriously turning on the tap, filling the sink with hot, sudsy water, piling the dirty pots and pans on the counter next to the sink, scraping the grease into the trash can, and then plunging the pots and pans into the sink. So the least I can do is scrub them.

As I scrub I think, *If in the future I ever hear anyone spouting off about how nice it would be to live in the olden days before electricity and labor-saving devices, I'll say to that person, "Wake up, lamebrain! Scrubbing pots is disgusting. You get hot and sweaty, your hair frizzes, your hands turn into shriveled prunes, and pretty soon you are greasier*

than the pots you're scrubbing. Really. I mean it. I know, be-cause I've been there, done that. So go into your kitchen and hug your dishwasher right now."

As we're scraping and scrubbing, Kit finds a thick slice of bacon stuck to one of the pans. She is about to slip it to Buddy when we see a little boy peeking at us through the back door, which is open. He clearly needs the bacon more than Buddy does. Kit gives it to him while I fill a cup with water for him at the sink. He eats, drinks, smiles a shy smile, and then disappears.

Except for the fact that I'm all slimy, I sort of like being behind the lunch counter because it's right in the main room of the general store, so we can peek over our shoulders and see and hear all the action. The bell over the door to the store rings cheerfully as custom-ers come in. They all call out to the owner, "Hello, Mrs. Finch!" They buy sugar and nails, apples and pickles, buttons and shoe polish. The wall on the side opposite the lunch counter is full of shelves stocked with mate-rial, which I would love to look at. To me, the materials are all dreamy, vintage stuff. But of course, they're just common, ordinary fabrics in the 1930s.

I'm drying a pot when I overhear a young woman

saying, "Oh, I just don't know which material I should buy! I'm making a suit."

"A suit?" says Mrs. Finch. "Where do you wear a suit in Lewis Falls, honey?"

I turn away from the sink and look at the young woman over the lunch counter just as Buddy trots over to greet her. "Doesn't she look like Ginger Rogers?" I ask Kit, naming a movie star from the 1930s.

Glancing over her shoulder, Kit smiles and nods in agreement.

"Hello, sweetie!" Ginger Rogers says to Buddy. Obviously smitten, she picks him up and snuggles him as she answers Mrs. Finch. "I just landed a job in Cincinnati. So I need to look tailored and businesslike. I don't want to look dowdy."

I see that Ginger Rogers is looking at two bolts of material. One is a floaty, flowered chiffon and the other is a navy blue serge. It's so clear to me which material she should choose that I'm practically exploding. Making outfits from the clothes I buy at secondhand stores has taught me a lot about fabrics. I think of what Kit said, about grabbing a chance when you see it. So even though I know it's nervy of me, I pipe up,

"Choose the navy. The chiffon will look too frilly for a business suit."

Mrs. Finch and Ginger Rogers smile in surprise, and Ginger Rogers says, "The navy it is!"

While Mrs. Finch is cutting the cloth for her, Ginger Rogers carries Buddy over to the lunch counter and says to Kit and me, "I'm excited about moving to Cincinnati. My job starts next week."

I poke Kit hard with my elbow—it's her turn to "grab the chance."

"If you need a place to live, my family has a boardinghouse in Cincinnati," says Kit. "It's clean and safe and not expensive. The food is good, too. I'm sure you'd be comfortable there." She grins and points to Buddy. "You've already made friends with one of our boarders."

"He's adorable," says Ginger Rogers. "I'm in love with him." She kisses Buddy and puts him on the floor. "And I do need a place to stay. My, but if you two aren't the most helpful girls in the world! Between the two of you, I'm all set. Thank you!"

Kit gives Ginger Rogers her home address and a neighbor's telephone number since the Kittredges don't

have a phone.

"May I thank you girls by buying you sandwiches?" asks Ginger Rogers. "And pie, too, if you like."

"Yes, please!" say Kit and I together. We finish the pots, dry our hands, and sit on stools at the lunch counter. Now granted, I have never been so hungry before, but oh, that sandwich and the pie that Ginger Rogers buys for me are the best I have ever eaten in my life! Ginger Rogers has to leave before we have finished eating, so Kit and I hop off our stools and shake hands with her, and Buddy demands one more kiss from her. Then we all say good-bye and thank you and see you soon. Ginger Rogers leaves, and Kit and I go back to eating our pie.

Mrs. Finch not only gives us as much milk as we want for free, but she also pays us for scrubbing the pots. You'd have to pay me a hundred bucks to scrub those pots again! But Mrs. Finch gives Kit and me two nickels each.

Kit is pleased. "Thank you, Mrs. Finch," she says. "I'm sure this is more than enough to buy our tickets back to Cincinnati."

When I hold my two nickels in my hand—the

still-pruney hand that worked so hard to scrub the pots clean—I feel that I've earned them so I deserve to keep them for myself. But the face of that poor little boy haunts me. I think of how kind Mrs. Finch was to Kit and me, and how Ginger Rogers bought us food, and I feel torn.

❧ *To give money to the hungry boy,*
   turn to page 149.

❧ *To buy train tickets to Cincinnati,*
   turn to page 158.

The woman grabs me by the arm. She reaches out to grab Kit, but as she turns I wrench my arm out of her grasp, take the front steps in a flying leap, and yell "Run!"

Kit takes off. I run as fast as I have ever run in my life, but I can't keep up with her. Luckily, the woman can't keep up with either of us, and we soon leave her far behind.

I follow Kit down the street and around a corner until we come to a park. We both slump onto the nearest park bench—panting, sweating, hearts pounding.

When I can talk, I say, "Sorry about losing Uncle Hendrick's letter."

"That's okay," says Kit. "That neighbor lady would probably have suspected us of stealing *it*, too."

"Why did she think we were hoboes?" I ask.

"Just because of the way we look," says Kit.

"And are hoboes bad?"

"No," Kit replies, "but lots of people don't trust them, even though it's not the hoboes' fault that they're homeless."

"That's terrible!" I sputter. "That's, like, totally unfair! That's—"

"—something that someone ought to do something about?" asks Kit, finishing my sentence.

"Yes!" I exclaim. But what?

I'm quiet as Kit and I walk back to her house. I can't stop thinking about how terrible it would feel to be truly homeless. "I think someone should write a letter to the newspaper about being kinder to homeless people," I finally blurt out.

"Me too," Kit agrees. "Do you want to use my typewriter?"

"Me?" I squeak, pointing to myself. "I'm not a good writer."

"All it takes to be a good writer is to have something you really want to say."

There's something about being with Kit that makes me feel as if I am capable of doing anything. I hear myself say, "Okay, after we find Buddy, I'll give the letter a try. But only if you'll help me. Deal?"

"Deal." Kit sticks out her hand, and we shake on it.

❧ *Turn to page 151.*

s I reach out to take Buddy from Kit's arms, Inky growls again. That gives me a great idea.

"Thank you for your invitation, Uncle Hendrick," I say, "but it looks as though my dog and your dog don't get along." *Thank you, stinky Inky,* I think to myself.

"That's right," says Kit, who gets it immediately. "So, Lulu had better not accept your gracious invitation. We'll just get her suitcase and go."

Grr, grumps Uncle Hendrick, in a pretty good imitation of Inky. "That preposterous puppy! Very well, then. There's so much disorder and chaos at the Kittredge house, one more flea-ridden addition to the menagerie won't be noticed. As for Lucille's suitcase, it isn't here yet. I'll have a taxi bring it up to your house when it arrives."

He leads Kit and Buddy and me back to the front hall, opens the door, and says, "Good-bye." He sounds as though he means, "Go! You've wasted enough of my precious time already!"

"Good-bye," Kit and I say.

As he closes the door behind us, Kit grins at me. "Phew," she says quietly.

"You can say that again. He's a real sourpuss, isn't he?"

Kit nods. "I never thought I would say this, but thank goodness for Inky! Come on, Lulu. You too, Buddy. Let's go home."

❊ *Turn to page 181.*

ey, Kit," I say, "I know this sounds crazy, but what if we give the money we earned to that hungry boy? He's even worse off than we are. Maybe we could call somebody to come get us, instead of taking the train." Then I remember Kit's family doesn't have a car—or a phone. "Is there anybody we could call and ask to come get us and give us a ride home?"

Kit makes a face. "We could call my Uncle Hendrick." She pronounces *Uncle Hendrick* as if she's saying *Count Dracula*. "He has a phone and a car. It'll be a collect call and he'll be really grouchy about it, but he'll come."

"Then I think that's what we should do," I say. "How about you?"

Kit nods. "I think so, too," she says.

We find the little boy sitting behind the back door, looking forlorn. His dirty face breaks into a gigantic smile when we give him our four nickels. I mean, he looks at us as if we're magicians or good fairies. I'll never forget the look on his face.

Then we go back inside the store and ask to use the phone to make a collect call.

"Now hold it just a minute!" Mrs. Finch calls out. "I saw what you did, you darlin' girls—giving all that

pot-scrubbing money to that poor little sad-sack boy. And don't I know better than anyone how hard earned that money was! How are you going to get home now that you've given away your train fare?"

Kit says, "We're going to call my uncle and beg him to come and get us."

"Not if I have anything to do about it!" says Mrs. Finch bossily. "Why, my husband is plannin' on drivin' to Cincinnati tomorrow. He can just as well drive this very afternoon, and give you two a ride."

And that is exactly what happens. Clearly, Mrs. Finch is the kind of person who gets her own way.

Kit and I hug her good-bye and then we climb in the back of an old pickup truck with Buddy. It's a bone-jouncing ride, but we love every minute of it. Mr. Finch drops us off at Union Station, and we walk home to the Kittredges' house, feeling very happy and very, very tired.

❈ *Turn to page 165.*

When Kit and I round the corner to her street, we see the most wonderful sight: Charlie is standing at the end of the front walk, and *Buddy is in his arms!* Kit and I break into a run and practically tackle Charlie to the ground, we are so happy to see Buddy.

"Buddy," I murmur. "I was afraid I'd lost you forever."

"I figured we'd find him eventually," says Kit.

"You didn't find him—he found you," Charlie points out. He grins and hands Buddy to me. "Buddy found his way home all by himself. He's one smart puppy!"

I can't talk because I am too busy smooching Buddy. Kit bounces up and down until I hand Buddy to her so that she can hug him, too.

After our joyful reunion with Buddy, we tell Charlie about our not-so-joyful adventures at Uncle Hendrick's house. I end by saying, "Uncle Hendrick's neighbor was mean to us just because of how we look. And people are mean to hoboes just because they look poor and bedraggled. It's not right."

Charlie nods. "One of my favorite authors, Henry David Thoreau, said, 'It's not what you look at that matters, it's what you see.' That woman, and others like her, don't see hoboes as people who deserve to be

respected no matter what their clothes look like."

Kit gives me a challenging grin. "Come on," she says. "Let's go write that letter."

"Ohh-kaay," I say reluctantly.

We go up to Kit's room. Kit rolls a piece of paper into her typewriter and looks at me expectantly. "You talk, I'll type," she says. "My typewriter is a little finicky."

I look at the blank paper and get the same sinking feeling that I always get when I look at a blank computer screen. "Argh!" I moan. "How do I start?"

"Well," says Kit, "first, state your opinion, and then back it up with facts. Start with 'I think' and then see how it goes from there."

I'm quiet for a while. Then I say, "I think it's wrong to be mean to hoboes. It's not *their* fault they're homeless."

"Good!" says Kit, clickety-clacking away as she types what I just said.

"Homelessness is something that could happen to anyone," I say, thinking of how close the Kittredges come every month to losing their home if they can't pay the mortgage. "So before you look at a hobo and think *tramp, bum, thief,* try to see the person. Put yourself in his or her shoes."

"Shoes that are probably falling apart and full of holes," Kit adds.

"That's good!" I say. "Type that, and then put, 'Instead of ignoring hoboes or judging them harshly, have sympathy for them, and compassion. The end.'"

"You don't put 'The end' on a letter to the editor," Kit says. "You put 'Sincerely yours,' and then write your name." She finishes typing the letter and rolls the paper out of the typewriter. "I'll go downstairs and get an envelope," she says, handing the letter to me. "Would you like to check this over?"

"Okay," I say. Then before she disappears down the stairs, impulsively I add, "Hey, Kit—thanks. You're a good writing partner."

Kit grins. "You're a good everything partner," she says.

As soon as she leaves, I fold the letter and put it in my pocket.

I feel sorrowful, but resolved. I've realized that, even though I sort of don't want to, the time has come for me to go home because—well, because maybe I can make a difference there.

I take a clean piece of paper and a pencil and write,

Dear Kit,
Thank you for the most unforgettable day of my life. Please take care of Buddy.
Love,
Me

Then I click the camera.

❈

Back in my own bedroom at home, I pull the letter out of my pocket. Turning on my laptop, I find the e-mail address of our local newspaper's 'Letters to the Editor' section.

I retype our letter, changing the word *hoboes* to *homeless people* because I'm not sure we still use the word *hobo* in the twenty-first century. As I type, I'm thinking about Kit and how pleased she would be, and how grateful I am to her. I'm grateful because I brought more than the letter home from my visit—I brought home a whole new idea of myself.

This is what I write:

To the editor:

I think it is wrong to be mean to homeless people. It is not their fault that they are homeless. Homelessness is something that could happen to anyone. So before you look at a homeless person and think tramp, bum, thief, try to see the person. Put yourself in his or her shoes—shoes that are probably falling apart and full of holes. Instead of ignoring homeless people or judging them harshly, have sympathy for them, and compassion.

Remembering what Kit told me, I add "Sincerely yours" and my name, and click *send*.

Closing my laptop, I look out the window. It's still night outside, but with my bedroom lights on I see my own reflection more clearly than the sparkling lights of the city below. I gaze thoughtfully at my reflection: I look the same, but I know I have changed inside. I think Kit would be proud of me, if she were here. And in a way, she'll always be with me from now on.

❈ *The End* ❈

To read this story another way and see how different choices lead to a different ending, turn back to page 8.

Thank you, Uncle Hendrick. I'd like to stay here," I say. My heart aches, but I know that Kit's family will benefit most if I stay with him. That way, Kit's family can have the money he'll pay them without the expense of feeding me.

I turn to Kit. "It was wonderful to meet you, Kit. Please thank your family for me."

Kit looks crestfallen. "Lulu—" she begins.

Quickly, I realize that I've got to make Kit think I'm staying for my own selfish reasons, to fool her into thinking that I'm staying because I want to, not because it'll be best for her and her family. If she knew my real reason for staying, she would feel terrible. So I put on a snobby voice and say, "There's more room for me here. I'll be more comfortable."

Kit looks confused and hurt.

"Off you go, Kit!" Uncle Hendrick orders. "And take that ill-behaved dog with you."

The crushed look on Kit's face almost makes me change my mind. As she turns and heads down the steps to the sidewalk, I know I'm seeing one of the best friends I've ever had walk away.

Buddy looks at me from over Kit's shoulder with

such a sad expression that I have to turn my head.

I know staying with Uncle Hendrick is best for the Kittredges, but that does not make it hurt any less.

❈ *Turn to page 164.*

K it sees my hesitation, and she hesitates, too. "How much will our tickets cost?" she asks Mrs. Finch.

"Kids pay half-fare," says Mrs. Finch, "so it'll be a nickel each."

Kit and I look at each other. "Are you thinking what I'm thinking?" Kit asks.

"About giving our other two nickels to that hungry boy?" I ask.

"Yes!" smiles Kit. "Let's do it."

Buddy comes outside with us and leaps and barks his sharp little puppy barks of happiness as we give two nickels to the hungry boy. The boy is so over-whelmed that he whispers, "Thanks," and his eyes fill with tears. As long as I live, I will never forget his grateful face—and for a mere *ten cents*. I make a vow never to take even the smallest gift for granted ever again.

Kit and Buddy and I walk to the train station in Lewis Falls and march right up to the ticket window.

"Two tickets to Cincinnati, please," says Kit, sound-ing very grown-up. I wish the railroad bulls could see us buying our tickets. I'd look down my nose at them.

No wonder they're called bulls—they're bullies!

When the train pulls into Lewis Falls with a whistle and clang and screech, I can't help but feel sort of excited and relieved at the same time. I carry Buddy aboard, and Kit and I sit on the rather scratchy seats. We look out the window all the way, and when we cross the bridge over the river so that we're back in Cincinnati, we grin at each other.

"Phew," says Kit.

"Seriously," I agree.

"Union Station!" shouts the conductor. Kit, Buddy, and I are the first ones off. The station is echoey and cavernous inside, full of hurrying people. It is so huge and beautiful that I feel as though I'm in a cathedral with a ceiling that arches up to heaven. But Kit and I don't dillydally. We are too eager to get home.

❋ *Turn to page 165.*

Uncle Hendrick's neighbor makes us lock the door, leaving the suitcase and hidden key behind. Then, as if we are lowlifes, she herds Kit and me down the tree-lined street. People stare at us as we pass by. It makes me feel so ashamed! In fact, it makes me feel as though we really *are* thieves. I've never been judged so harshly, so unfairly, so quickly—and all just because of my clothes! I ask myself if I've ever judged anyone in this way, and promise myself that I never will again.

The woman ushers us past a giant railroad station, past the rail yards, to the edge of a river. A scraggly grassed slope descends to a bushy area under a trestle bridge. She points to a grove of trees and low shrubs near the foot of the trestles, and I can see that there's a cleared-out space with a smoky fire in the middle of it.

"Go down there, back where you belong," the woman says. "And don't let me catch you sneaking up to where decent folks live or trying to beg food at a soup kitchen, either. You stay put in the jungle, or better yet, get out of town. If I see you again, I'll take you to the police."

She stands at the top of the slope, arms crossed over her chest, and watches us walk down toward the trees by the trestle. Then she marches off.

As we approach the campfire, a thin, stooped old man comes up to us. "Young gals, what are y'all doing here?"

Kit and I exchange a glance. "A lady thought we were hoboes," Kit explains. "So she made us come here."

The man smiles. "Well, I can see that you ain't hoboes," he says. "I can also see that y'all are hot, hungry, and tired. So sit down in the shade, and I'll fetch you some water."

Kit and I sit in the shade of a little tree. There are some falling-down shacks—really, just boards leaning against trees or other boards—and a few tattered and filthy tents. Some people are washing clothes in the river, and others are talking, reading, or eating something from a pot over the fire. Babies cry, a man strums a guitar, and I hear a group of girls playing jump rope and chanting jump-rope rhymes.

The old man brings us washed-out tin cans full of water. He's like the exact opposite of Uncle Hendrick's neighbor. His kindness is another reminder that it's a mistake to judge people by appearances. Kit and I thank him, and Kit tries to give him a nickel.

The man shakes his head. "You best keep your nickel, Miss," he tells Kit. "Y'all may need it to help you get safe home."

I touch the camera. I don't need a nickel to get "safe home" to the twenty-first century. But there's no way I'd leave Kit right now.

We finish our water, thank the kind man again, and walk back up the hill to the railroad tracks.

"I think we do need that nickel to get home safely," Kit says, looking serious. "That lady said if she saw us again, she'd take us to the police. We'd better use the nickel to call Charlie and ask him to walk us home, in case we run into that lady."

Kit and I walk to the train station. It's called Union Station and it's humongous—and beautiful. It makes me think of a palace in *The Arabian Nights.* Wide steps lead up to fountains in front of the enormous doors, and the arched front is sky-high. Inside, the walls are decorated with murals that show the history of Cincinnati.

Kit leads me to the phone booths—which fascinate me because we don't have them in my twenty-first-century town—and we use the nickel to call her next-

door neighbors' house. "We don't have a phone any-more," Kit explains to me, as she waits for someone to answer. "We can't afford it. I hope Mrs. Lucero answers her phone. Normally, I'd call my friend Ruthie, but she and her family are still away."

I can't imagine being without a phone! Most people I know carry a cell phone all the time and are never out of calling distance.

"Mrs. Lucero?" Kit says into the phone. "This is Kit Kittredge. Please, I need your help. I'm at Union Station. Can you ask Charlie to come walk me home?" She listens, and then says, "Thank you very much, Mrs. Lucero. Good-bye." Kit hangs up and then says to me, "Charlie will be on his way soon."

I'm relieved but embarrassed, too. This whole mess is my fault. If only I hadn't lost Uncle Hendrick's letter! I hate to look like Loony Lulu in front of Cool Cute Charlie.

❦ *Turn to page 168.*

After Kit and Buddy leave, Uncle Hendrick says, "If you want anything to eat, go to the kitchen and help yourself. Don't come pestering me." Then he leaves, too, and I am all alone.

I walk into the room full of books. It smells of dust, and the air seems old and still, as if there hasn't been a window open or a fresh breeze blowing through in a hundred years. It's weird—the room looks nothing like the living room in our apartment at home, but the way everything is so quiet, somehow it sort of *feels* the same.

Or maybe it's just me. *I* feel the same as I do at home: lonely. Maybe I might as well *go* home. Kit's family will have the money they need—at least for this month's mortgage. They can take care of Buddy, and Buddy can be Grace's pal. I can't help the Kittredges anymore—or can I? Maybe I should stay and see what happens.

❈ *To go home now,*
 turn to page 170.

❈ *To stay at Uncle Hendrick's house,*
 turn to page 176.

Back at the Kittredges' house, everyone is in a state of high excitement.

"Lulu, I'm so glad you came back with Kit," says Mrs. Kittredge, "because I want to thank both of you together. Our neighbor told me that there was a call for me on her telephone, so I went over, and I spoke to a very nice young woman who wants to rent a room in our house. She said you two told her about it."

Kit and I exchange a happy glance. "Ginger Rogers," we say in unison.

"The young woman is not only willing to share a room with you, Kit, she says she won't mind sharing with Buddy," says Mrs. Kittredge. "She says it was love at first sight between Buddy and her. She'll move in next week!"

"That's great news!" says Kit.

"A new boarder is a new source of income," says Mr. Kittredge. He smiles at Kit and me. "Thanks to you girls, we'll be able to pay the mortgage this month."

"Lulu, you are welcome to stay as long as you like," says Mrs. Kittredge. "Our family is grateful to you. Thank you."

"You're welcome!" I say. Then, leaving the Kittredges

to celebrate together, I go upstairs with Buddy.

Kit has told me that her room is at the very top of the house, in the attic, so Buddy and I keep going up until we can't go up anymore. Kit's room is tucked under the eaves and has four big windows that stick out. It's cozy and airy at the same time. Buddy jumps up onto the bed and immediately goes to sleep. I smile at him with love; he looks so comfortable and so at home, as if he's just part of the family now.

Family. Kit has taught me a whole new idea of what a family is. The Kittredges opened their house and their hearts and created a different kind of family. They welcomed their boarders, they welcomed Buddy and me, and now they're welcoming Ginger Rogers to join in—like a family—so that together they can make the best of their situation.

What about *my* family? It's just Mom and me, but maybe we could work together to make the best of *our* situation, too. I could work at it, that's for sure, maybe by thinking of things for Mom and me to do together, for example.

I hear a burst of laughter from downstairs. Buddy hears it, too, and wakes up and pricks up his ears.

"Buddy," I say, with a combination of sorrow and excitement, "it's time for me to go home. You'll be fine here with the Kittredges and your new friend, Ginger Rogers. I love you, and I'll miss you—and Kit—forever."

Quickly, before I can change my mind, I write Kit a note to say thank you and good-bye. I'm trembling a little as I pick up the camera, take one last look through the old-fashioned viewfinder at Kit's cool attic room, and click the button.

❧ *Turn to page 172.*

Union Station is a bustling place. The long wooden benches are crowded with people, and other people hurry by, rushing to catch trains and buses or running to hug people they've come to meet.

Kit and I are pretty happy to see Charlie coming to meet *us*.

Kit hugs him. "Oh, Charlie," she says, "you won't believe what happened to us."

Charlie shakes his head. "Probably not," he agrees. "But tell me anyway. I'm sure it's a great story!" He grins at me. "In fact, I bet it's a lulu."

We all laugh. See, Harry Sharma? It's possible for a guy to be nice looking *and* nice.

"I have good news, girls," Charlie continues. "Guess who found his way home all by himself?"

Kit and I gasp. Smiles light up our tired faces as we realize what Charlie means. "BUDDY!" we shout joyfully.

Charlie laughs. "Yup. And guess who is taking loving care of him right now? Mrs. Howard."

"Yikes," says Kit. "We'd better hurry home!"

She's surprised, but I'm not. I knew Buddy would make Mrs. Howard fall in love with him sooner or

later! Knowing that Buddy is now a one-hundred-percent-welcome member of the Kittredges' household is a relief, because it resolves a nagging worry I've had about who will care for Buddy when I leave.

Thinking about Kit's household makes me miss mine. I feel a funny tug at my heart when I think of Mom, and suddenly I realize that I'm longing for home. So just as Kit, Charlie, and I are about to leave the cool depths of Union Station and walk out into the sunshine, I stop.

❉ *Turn to page 173.*

I look around Uncle Hendrick's library for a piece of paper and a pencil. Finding both on his desk, I write Uncle Hendrick a note:

Dear Uncle Hendrick,
    Thank you for inviting me to visit. I have decided to go home.
Best wishes,
Your visitor

(I don't want to forge Lulu's name. Besides, maybe the real Lucille will show up soon. I love the idea of Uncle Hendrick going crazy trying to figure out who on earth I could have been!)

But I hate the idea of parting from Kit and leaving Kit feeling hurt and sad. So I write her a note, too:

Dear Kit,
    I stayed at Uncle Hendrick's because I thought it would be the best thing for you and your family—not because I didn't want to stay with you. I did!
    Now I am going home, but I can't leave without thanking you for being my friend, and for changing the way I see

everything in the whole world—including myself.
Your friend forever,
Me
P.S. I know Buddy will be happy with you and Grace and
your family. Thank you for taking care of him.

I fold the note and write on the outside of it,

Uncle Hendrick, please give this to Kit.

Then I click the camera.

❄ *Turn to page 174.*

'm sitting on my bed when the door opens. It's Mom.

"Hi, sweetie. You look lost in thought," she says. "What's on your mind?"

"You and me," I say.

"That's funny," says Mom, "because I've been thinking about us, too." She sits on my bed and kicks off her high heels.

"Mom," I say, "wouldn't it be fun for us to go somewhere together this weekend, just the two of us?"

"Yes, it would," says Mom. "You'd really like that?"

I fling my arms around her as my answer.

Mom laughs. "I'll take that as a yes," she says. "And you and I have a lot to talk about. For instance, do you think it's time to add another member to our family?"

I pull back and look at her.

She says, "Maybe a small, furry, roly-poly—"

"*Puppy!*" we say together.

❀ *The End* ❀

To read this story another way and see how different choices lead to a different ending, turn back to page 8.

K it," I say, "I think I should go home now."

Kit nods. "We'll be home soon."

"No." My throat is tight as I say it. "I mean *home* home—*my* home. I really miss my mother. I, um, I can use my return ticket from the, uh, train station here." It's not a lie—the camera *is* my ticket home. "And Buddy will be happy with Mrs. Howard to care for him."

Kit looks at me searchingly. Suddenly, she hugs me hard. "It was wonderful to meet you, Lulu," she says. "I will never, ever forget you."

"Neither will I," adds Charlie. "You'll always be the lulu-liest Lulu I've ever known."

"I'll never forget you two, either," I say, trying (and failing) to smile. "Thanks for everything."

Kit's eyes are full of tears. She whispers, "You're welcome." And then she and Charlie leave.

I watch them walk away—Charlie's arm slung over Kit's shoulder to comfort her—until I can't see them anymore. Then I click the camera, and go home.

❈ *Turn to page 179.*

t home, in my room, I think about how sometimes you have to let go of someone or something you love because it is best for that person. Like, I did not want to leave Kit, but I did anyway because it was best for her family. I wonder—is that the most important idea I learned this summer? I open my laptop and start to write my essay.

I haven't been writing long before Mom comes in.

"Hi, sweetheart," she says, looking tired. "Sorry I'm so late."

Usually, I would be sulky and nag Mom about how she's never home, and whine about how bored and lonely I've been. But I have learned from Kit not to be selfish. "That's okay, Mom," I say. "I know you've had a long day. I'm just really glad to see you now."

"Thanks, honey," says Mom. She looks pleased, but a little surprised, too.

I give Mom a hug and tell her, "I know I don't say it much, but I appreciate how hard you work." With the memory fresh in my mind of how Kit helped her mother with the boardinghouse, I add, "Could I ever come with you to the lab where you work, to see what it's like?"

Now Mom looks really surprised, but she says, "Yes! I'd love to show you around. Maybe when school starts, you could come to my office every Friday afternoon after school and hang out, and then we could go out for dinner. That way, we could spend more time together. What do you say?"

"Sounds like a good plan."

"Come on," says Mom. "I'll make us a cup of mint tea, and we'll have a nice talk. You can tell me what you've done today."

"Okay, you got it," I say with a grin. "You won't *believe* how interesting today was!"

❧ The End ❧

To read this story another way and see how different choices lead to a different ending, turn back to page 164.

I sit in a giant chair and pull a book off the shelf. I love to read, and anyway, there's nothing else to do. There's no TV, and no computer. The book is thick and the print is small, and some of the words are too hard, but pretty soon I'm caught up in the story. It's called *Pride and Prejudice*, and it's about five sisters. They remind me of Izza and her sisters, because they're sort of funny and lively.

I'm surprised when Uncle Hendrick appears. I decide I've got nothing to lose, so I'm friendly. "Hi," I say, looking up from my book with a smile.

Uncle Hendrick just sniffs. "Isn't that book too difficult for you?"

"A little bit," I admit. "But I like it."

"Hmph," says Uncle Hendrick. "So you like to read?"

"Oh, yes," I say. "I love it."

Uncle Hendrick gets a funny look on his face. It takes me a while to realize what it is: he's smiling.

We talk about books for a bit, and then Uncle Hendrick says, "I don't suppose . . . no, probably not."

"What?" I ask.

"Do you play backgammon?" Uncle Hendrick asks.

"Do I play backgammon?" I repeat. "Is Roosevelt

the president of the United States?"

At this, Uncle Hendrick laughs. It sounds like tires on gravel, but he's definitely laughing. He dusts off an ancient backgammon board, and we begin to play. I'm good, but he's better. He beats me twice, but it's really fun anyway.

As we play, I think, *I'm glad I reached out a little bit to Uncle Hendrick. He's not so bad after all.*

Maybe I had to come to the 1930s to learn that if you try to engage with someone, you can make a friend out of even the most unlikely prospect. I kind of feel like a coconut has bounced on my head when I realize the very next moment, *Hey, maybe I could make friends with my babysitter.* Maybe Sophie's sort of like Uncle Hendrick, and I just need to put out some effort and try to make friends with her.

I decide there and then that when I return home, I will invite my babysitter to play a game with me. Who knows? Maybe she's a backgammon star, like Uncle Hendrick. Or maybe she likes movies, or doing yoga, or karaoke. No matter what, we'll have fun together, and I won't be lonely every day after school when I come home.

Uncle Hendrick sees me smile. "I wouldn't look so happy if I were you," he says. "I've just won again."

"You know what, Uncle Hendrick?" I say with a grin. "I think we've *both* won."

❈ *The End* ❈

To read this story another way and see how different choices lead to a different ending, turn back to page 138.

I find myself sitting on the floor of my room. Everything is just the same as before, with my clothes and books and sports equipment all tossed in heaps. I guess I just see it differently now: my room looks worse than just messy and disorganized—it looks careless and thoughtless, as if I'm so spoiled that I don't value any of my belongings.

I think of how little Kit had, and how some of the people Kit and I saw had *nothing,* and I blush, ashamed. Then I set to work to clean up my room. I hang up my clothes, I put my books on the shelf, I put my sports equipment in the closet. Soon there is only one thing left to put away: the camera. What would happen if I clicked it again? Would it send me back to Kit, or to some other completely different time and place? I've got to find out. With a mixture of jittery curiosity and hope, I click the camera.

What happens? Nothing. I am still home. *That's right, camera,* I think. *I've had a tremendous and wonderful adventure with Kit. No need to be greedy.*

Gently, I put the camera back in the box with the secondhand clothes, back where I first found it. Then I go into the kitchen and make a nice snack of apples and

cheese for Mom. It's waiting for her when she comes home from work.

"Well, this is nice, sweetie!" Mom says, setting down her briefcase and drawing me into a hug. "I'm grateful."

I hug Mom back. "I'm the one who's grateful," I tell her, resolving to show Mom how grateful I am, every day from now on, by taking care of my belongings. But words will have to do for now. "Mom, thanks for all that you've given me. Thanks for *everything*."

❄ *The End* ❄

To read this story another way and see how different choices lead to a different ending, turn back to page 134.

W hen Kit and I arrive back at her house, we go upstairs to her bedroom in the attic, where Grace is waiting for us. Kit starts to polish her shoes—which I've never seen anyone actually do before. Absentmindedly, I pull a book off of Kit's bookshelf. *"The Wonderful Wizard of Oz!"* I say. "I love that movie!"

Kit looks puzzled. "Movie?" she asks.

Ooops—time travel blooper. I guess the famous movie of *The Wizard of Oz* hasn't been made yet. "Uh, I mean *book,*" I say quickly. "I love it when Dorothy taps the heels of her magic slippers together and says, 'There's no place like home.'"

"Me too," says Kit. She laughs and closes her eyes and bonks together the heels of the brown oxford shoes that she is polishing. "There's no place like home. There's no place like home," she chants. Then she opens her eyes. "Hey, look!" she says. "It worked. I'm home."

I laugh and open the book eagerly. I haven't been reading long when Stirling appears. "Hi," he says. "Kit, here's the picture you asked me to draw." He hands Kit a sheet of paper with some typing and drawing on it. I look at it over Kit's shoulder.

"Whoa!" I say. Stirling's drawing is just a pencil

sketch of Buddy and me looking at each other, but Stirling's caught that impish look in Buddy's eyes, and my expression shows how much I love Buddy. "This is really good."

"It sure is," says Kit. "Thanks, Stirling."

Stirling blushes. I can tell he's pleased.

"Would you like to see some of the old newsletters Stirling and Ruthie and I used to make?" Kit asks.

"Yes!" I say.

Kit drags a box out from under her desk, and I plop on the floor. But before I begin to look through it, I have an inspiration. "Hey, Stirling, while I look at these, would you draw a sketch of Kit and Buddy and Grace for me?" I ask.

"Sure," says Stirling. He whips a pencil out of his back pocket, takes a piece of paper off Kit's desk, and goes right to work. Kit sits on the floor and continues to polish her shoes, which is tough to do with Buddy curled up in her lap. When Grace tries to fit onto Kit's lap, too, Kit and Stirling laugh. I can see that they are really good friends. Watching them laugh together makes me miss *my* good friend Izza.

I open the box. One of the newsletters announces

that Stirling and his mother are coming to live with the Kittredges. Another newsletter is designed like a "Help Wanted" advertising page from when Kit's family was first setting up their boardinghouse. One ad says,

Wanted! Kids with wagon to haul away leftover lumber suitable for use in fixing sleeping porch. Call Ruthie Smithens.

Another ad says,

Talented handyman to fix sleeping porch so it will sleep two. Great working conditions! Call the Kittredge family.

Then there are some funny advice columns. One girl wrote to say that Rotten Roger was stealing her lunch every day. Kit's advice column said,

Bring an extra lunch bag of dried-up leaves and let Rotten Roger take that bag. Put in a note that says, "I have a hunch you'll munch and crunch this lunch a bunch!"

I'm laughing at Kit's advice when Mrs. Howard comes up the stairs calling, "Stirling? Lamby? Are you up here?"

At the sound of her voice—the voice of his true love—Buddy jumps to his feet, flies across the room, and gazes up at her with big brown puppy-dog eyes. And to my surprise, Mrs. Howard kneels down, lifts Buddy up, and gives him a hug and a kiss. Her face is transformed from being nervous and tight to looking open and happy. I just have to smile at her, and she smiles warmly back at me.

"Lulu," Mrs. Howard says slowly, "when you first arrived, I thought your dog was a bother. I was wrong, and I'm sorry."

"No worries," I say. "That's okay." And it really is okay. In fact, I can see that I was wrong about Mrs. Howard. I thought she was resistant to Buddy's irresistibility, and what kind of person wouldn't adore a sweet, happy-go-lucky puppy like Buddy? But now I know she's just as nice and softhearted as anybody.

Gently, reluctantly, Mrs. Howard puts Buddy down. Kit, Stirling, and I sneak knowing looks at one another, and I can tell we're all thinking the same thing: Buddy

has obviously completely won Mrs. Howard's heart. She is his new best friend.

Then Mrs. Howard says, "Stirling, dear, it's time for your cold medicine. And Kit, your mother needs you to help in the vegetable garden."

I put the newsletters away in the box and pick up *The Wonderful Wizard of Oz.* "Is it okay if I stay up here and read?" I ask Kit.

"Sure," she says.

As soon as Kit, Stirling, Mrs. Howard, Grace, and Buddy leave, I settle back into the reading chair. But I can't stop thinking about my home, and my friend Izza. Just as Dorothy met people she loved in Oz but still longed for Kansas, I love being with Kit and Buddy, but I am suddenly overwhelmed with longing for my own home and longing to spend time with my mother and my friend Isabel.

I wonder if Mom would let Isabel come home with me after school this year. Izza would appreciate the peace and quiet to do homework in, and I would appreciate the fun of her company.

Suddenly, I'm eager to go home and ask Mom. I find a scrap of paper and write Kit a note:

Dear Kit,

Seeing your copy of The Wizard of Oz reminded me that "There's no place like home." My visit with you was as magical as Dorothy's trip to Oz. Because of you, like Dorothy I learned that good friends bring us joy and also help us through tough times. And because of you, like the Tin Man, the Scarecrow, and the Cowardly Lion, I've learned to use my heart, my brain, and my courage to face scary situations.

I am going home now, but I will never forget you or Buddy. By the way, you know who I think will take good care of Buddy? His new best friend, Mrs. Howard!

Love,

Me

I set my note on top of *The Wonderful Wizard of Oz*. Stirling has left his sketch of Kit, Buddy, and Grace on Kit's desk, so I fold it carefully and put it in my pocket. I don't have magic slippers to knock together, but I do have the camera. I click it, and the next thing I know, I am home.

❉ *The End* ❉

To read this story another way and see how different choices lead to a different ending, turn back to page 105.

ABOUT Kit's Time

Kit Kittredge is a fictional character, but her story tells about a real time. In the 1930s, when Kit was growing up, America had fallen into the Great Depression. Some families escaped the hard times at first, but as the years went by, the Depression drove many businesses to shut down, putting millions of people out of work. Without jobs, people did not have the money to buy enough food, clothing, or other essentials. A family who could not pay their mortgage could easily lose their home.

Thousands of Americans did lose their homes and started to wander the country in search of work and a place to live. They were known as *tramps* or *hoboes*. More than half of these wanderers were teenagers or children. Some teenagers left home so that their families would have one less mouth to feed; others simply had nowhere else to go.

Hoboes developed their own special language of symbols, which they marked on houses, fences, and sidewalks to tell other hoboes what they might find. They traveled mostly by walking, but when they could, they sneaked onto trains without a ticket, sometimes riding in boxcars so they wouldn't be seen.

Riding the rails was dangerous. Hoboes sometimes jumped on or off while the train was moving, and railroad *bulls*, or guards, might use violence to discourage hoboes from riding the rails. But not everyone treated hoboes harshly. Many people gave them food or even payment in exchange for chores (as the woman at the lunch counter does in the story) or handed down clothes that they no longer needed.

In 1932, Americans elected a new president who they believed would pull the country out of the Depression—an optimistic man named Franklin Roosevelt. He had pledged to deliver "a New Deal for the American people," and after he became president, he launched new programs to put people back to work and pull the country out of its slump.

Skeptics like Uncle Hendrick, who thought that the poor had caused their own problems through laziness, didn't approve of President Roosevelt or his programs, but most Americans did—and they re-elected him three times. (Uncle Hendrick would have lost the bet Lulu made with him!)

Like Kit, girls growing up in the 1930s learned to be thrifty. They worked hard to help their families make ends meet and dreamed up creative ways to make their own clothes—and their own fun. Long before the word *recycle* was in common use, families like the Kittredges were recycling almost everything. A popular motto was: *Use it up, wear it out, make it do, or do without.* Resourceful girls like Kit learned to have fun without spending money, and everyone appreciated and treasured what money couldn't buy—the kindness and generosity of friends, family, and strangers, too.

Read more of KIT'S stories,

available from booksellers and at *americangirl.com*

❋ *Classics* ❋
Kit's classic series, now in two volumes:

Volume 1:
Read All About It!
Kit has a nose for news. When
the Great Depression hits
home, Kit's newsletters begin
making a real impact.

Volume 2:
Turning Things Around
With Dad still out of work,
Kit wonders if things will ever
get better. Could a letter to the
newspaper make a difference?

❋ *Journey in Time* ❋
Travel back in time—and spend a day with Kit!

Full Speed Ahead
Help Kit outwit Uncle Hendrick, find a missing puppy, and stay
out of jail when she's caught riding a freight train like a hobo! You
get to choose your own path though this multiple-ending story.

❋ *Mysteries* ❋
More thrilling adventures with Kit!

Intruders at Rivermead Manor
What's really going on in the old mansion next door?

Missing Grace
Kit's beloved basset hound has disappeared without a trace.

A Thief in the Theater
Can Kit catch the thief before the theater closes its doors for good?

Danger at the Zoo
With her reporter's instinct, Kit sniffs out some monkey business!

❀ *A Sneak Peek at* ❀

Read All About It!

A Kit Classic

Volume 1

Kit's adventures continue in the
first volume of her classic stories.

ounding the typewriter keys as hard as she could made Kit feel better. The good thing about writing was that she got to tell the whole story without anyone interrupting or contradicting her. Kit was pleased with her article when it was finished. It explained exactly what had happened and how the teacup was broken. Then at the end it said:

```
Sometimes a person is trying to do
something nice for another person and
it turns XXX out sadly badly by mistake
When ssomething bad happens and it isn'
my anyone's fault, no one should be
blamea. It's not fair!
```

Kit pulled her article out of the typewriter and marched outside to sit on the steps and wait for Dad to come home. She brought her book about Robin Hood to read while she waited.

She had not been reading long before the screen door squeaked open and slammed shut behind her. Kit didn't even lift her eyes off the page.

Charlie sat next to her. "Hi," he said.

Kit didn't answer. She was a little put out with

Charlie for adding to the trouble in Stirling's room.

"What's eating you, Squirt?" Charlie asked.

"Nothing," said Kit as huffily as she could.

Charlie looked at the piece of paper next to Kit. "Is that one of your newspapers for Dad?" he asked.

"Yup," said Kit.

Charlie picked up Kit's newspaper and looked at the headline. "'It's Not Fair,'" he read aloud. Then he asked, "What's this all about?"

"It's about how it's wrong to blame people for things that are not their fault," said Kit. "For example, *me*, for the mess this afternoon."

"Aw, come on, Kit," said Charlie. "That's nothing. You shouldn't make such a big deal of it."

"That's easy for *you* to say!" she said.

Charlie took a deep breath in and then let it out. "Listen, Kit," he said, in a voice that was suddenly serious, "I wouldn't bother Dad with this newspaper today if I were you."

Kit slammed her book shut and looked sideways at Charlie. "And why not?" she asked.

Charlie glanced over his shoulder to be sure that no one except Kit would hear him. "You know how lots of

people have lost their jobs because of the Depression, don't you?" he asked.

"Sure," said Kit. "Like Mr. Howard."

"Well," said Charlie, "yesterday Dad told Mother and me that he's closing down his car dealership and going out of business."

"*What*?" said Kit. She was horrified. "But . . ." she sputtered. "But *why*?"

"Why do you think?" said Charlie. "Because nobody has money to buy a car anymore. They haven't for a long time now."

"Well how come Dad didn't say anything before this?" Kit asked.

"He didn't want us to worry," said Charlie. "And he kept hoping things would get better if he just hung on. He didn't even fire any of his salesmen. He used his own savings to keep paying their salaries."

"What's Dad going to do now?" asked Kit.

"I don't know," said Charlie. "He even has to give back his own car. He can't afford it anymore. I guess he'll look for another job, though that's pretty hopeless these days."

Kit was sure that Charlie was wrong. "Anyone can

see that Dad's smart and hardworking!" she said. "And
he has so many friends! People still remember him
from when he was a baseball star in college. Plenty of
people will be glad to hire him!"

Charlie shrugged. "There just aren't any jobs to be
had. Why do you think people are going away?"

"Dad's not going to leave like Mr. Howard did!"
said Kit, struck by that terrible thought. Then she was
struck by another terrible thought. "We're not going to
lose our house like the Howards, are we?"

"I don't know," said Charlie again.

Kit could hardly breathe.

"It'll be a struggle to keep it," said Charlie. "Dad
told me that he and Mother don't own the house completely. They borrowed money from the bank to buy
it, and they have to pay the bank back a little every
month. It's called a mortgage. If they don't have enough
money to pay the mortgage, the bank can take the
house back."

"Well, the people at the bank won't just kick us out
onto the street, will they?" asked Kit.

"Yes," said Charlie. "That's exactly what they'll do.
You've seen those pictures in the newspapers of whole

families and all their belongings out on the street with nowhere to go."

"That is not going to happen to us," said Kit fiercely. "It's *not*."

"I hope not," said Charlie.

"Listen," said Kit. "How come Dad told Mother and *you* about losing his job, but not *me*?"

Charlie sighed a huge, sad sigh. "Dad told me," he said slowly, "because it means that I won't be able to go to college."

"Oh, Charlie!" wailed Kit, full of sympathy and misery. She knew that Charlie had been looking forward to college so much! And now he couldn't go. "That's terrible! That's awful! It's not *fair*."

Charlie grinned a cheerless grin and tapped one finger on Kit's newspaper. "That's your headline, isn't it?" he said. "These days a lot of things happen that aren't fair. There's no one to blame, and there's nothing that can be done about it." Charlie's voice sounded tired, as if he'd grown old all of a sudden. "You better get used to it, Kit. Life's not like books. There's no bad guy, and sometimes there's no happily ever after, either."

At that moment, Kit felt an odd sensation. Things were happening so fast! It was as if a match had been struck inside her and a little flame was lit, burning like anger, flickering like fear. "Charlie," she asked. "What's going to happen to us?"

"I don't know," said Charlie. He stood up to go.

"Wait," said Kit. "How come you told me about Dad? Was it just to stop me from bothering Dad with my newspaper?"

"No," said Charlie. "No. I told you because . . ." He paused. "Because you're part of this family, and I figured you deserve to know."

"Thanks, Charlie," said Kit. She was grateful to Charlie for treating her like a grown-up. "I'm glad you told me," she said, "even though I wish none of it were true."

"Me, too," said Charlie. "Me, too."

After Charlie left, Kit sat on the step thinking. No wonder Dad had not been happy about the Howards coming to stay. He must have been worried about more mouths to feed. And no wonder Mother had been short-tempered today. When she said that even though it was nobody's fault, they were still in a mess, she

must have been thinking of Dad. It wasn't his fault that they'd fallen into the terrible, slippery hole of the Depression, and yet, and yet . . . it surely seemed as though they had. Just like the Howards. Just like the kids at school. Just like the people she'd read about in the newspaper.

❋

About the Author

VALERIE TRIPP says that she became
a writer because of the kind of person she is.
She says she's curious, and writing requires
you to be interested in everything. Talking
is her favorite sport, and writing is a way of
talking on paper. She's a daydreamer, which
helps her come up with her ideas. And she
loves words. She even loves the struggle
to come up with just the right words as
she writes and rewrites. Ms. Tripp lives in
Maryland with her husband.

K